An 80's Dark Monster Horror Romance Comedy

YD LA MAR

BLURB

Life had always felt like a never-ending loop of expectations and rules. That's why when I spotted the "Help Wanted" sign at The Good Char, the hotdog on a stick food place in the mall. It was perfect! Like the condiments were calling my name. Little did I know, stepping into that vibrant hotdog stand would lead me straight into hell.

Dzik, my grumpy manager with an air of mystery about him, brooded and grumbled even after he hired me. His standoffish ways made me curious, even as his sharp wit tested my patience. As I served customers and wielded the tongs, a slow realization dawned on me—there was something different about this place, something beyond the ordinary.

With each passing day, I found myself fascinated by Dzik's gruff exterior. There was something more to him, something hidden and intriguing. Through the grease-splattered aprons and shared moments at the grill, I caught glimpses of it.

Then I found out what it was.

He's a demon, banished from the underworld,
working as my manager.

Now I'm not sure which of us is actually being
punished.

COURTESY WARNING

This book may contain triggers for some. Triggers include but are not limited to implied torture, gore, murder, violence, dismemberment, butchering of human flesh, explicit sex scenes, somnophilia, Asian parents, and consumption of human flesh.

Ranks **Dark Grey** on my personal darkness scale.

CHAPTER 1

DZIK

"Do you have any other options? Like, maybe a crunchy outside?" the kid with the boils on his face asked. He turned to his friend and continued. "The last time I went to the county fair, I got this really good deep fried one. Dude, it was the best corndog I ever had."

Pimples, my mind supplied. Humans called it pimples, not boils. Bah, it was all the same. Whatever it was, our demon of infection back home, Sabnock, did a better job than what I was looking at.

I leaned over the smooth, white counter, my nails raking the inside of my palms as I stared into the boy's face. "The menu above my head is all we have at The Good Char. You'll be guaranteed to not leave here wanting. We use only the best selected meats for our products."

The boy's face turned splotchy as if diseased and I leaned back and crossed my arms wondering if Sabnock was playing tricks on me. Humans were a strange lot and if it wasn't for the fact that I had a little too much fun back in the underworld, I wouldn't have been banished to this wretched place they called a mall. The name was false advertisement—Hellscape Mall indeed.

And who didn't like messing with the damned souls back home? It wasn't entirely my fault one of them somehow figured out how to escape back to the realm of men. It just so happened that the Master had also been moody lately and I inadvertently was in his path of destruction.

"Yeah, you're probably not going to get a deep fried corndog here. Just get something, you're holding up the line, Henry!" the friend exclaimed sheepishly, bringing me back to my current sorry existence.

Second hand embarrassment. It was a common trait among humans I came to find, though it still didn't make much sense why anyone would care what others were feeling. Dead or being tortured, their feelings had no attachments to the other being.

"All right, all right. I'll have the GC special, please," the boy finally chose with false exasperation.

A large, menacing grin split across my face before I made my way over to the grill—a vortex to the underworld. But to the humans, it was how we got our *good char.*

I worked alone once again after our last staff fell into the vortex from tripping over the recently cleaned floor—one that *he* mopped. Daniel never did watch what he was doing and created more work than necessary. Wasn't the point of hiring help...to get help? Luck was on my side that he wouldn't be missed. Daniel was a lone wolf, one that didn't have any family that cared. Not that any of that mattered, he was a crap employee. Good riddance, I say.

Spearing the meat and dipping it in our secret batter, I made my way over to our fryer and plunged it into its own personal hell and torture. Once it was satisfactory, I pulled the sizzling product out and placed it on its flimsy paper tray, handing it over to the resident of Death Canyon City.

Their eyes widened comically and I could practically see their mouths foaming for the delectable prize in their hands as I rang them up, then stood there with my arms crossed once more. This little prison of mine sported a trio of colors as the theme to match the other deplorable food stalls beside us. The red, yellow and deep purples made me want to wretch into the batter but being manager of The Good Char had its perks.

Customers were sparse this early in the day. Being the last stop on the food line also had that effect. The store beside us recently went under renovations, the construction leading most of our customers away.

I stood there with my chin in hand, pondering if I truly needed another worker to join my never ending torture. When more of the human teenagers looked over to my corner as the day went on, I curled my lip into a snarl, anticipating their jabbering and wishy-washy tendencies when ordering.

Yes, I needed another worker before I ended up inadvertently killing one of the customers from sheer annoyance. I let out a resigned sigh as I bent over and pulled out the 'now hiring' sign and placed it against one of the glass sneeze guards. Master help me, if I come across one more incompetent worker...

Leaning back against the opposite counter, I watch as the gaggle of teenage girls stroll past the construction—right for The Good Char.

"Oh! I haven't had a good corndog in so long! Let's get some!" one of the girls screeched. She stood a few heads shorter than me, with large framed glasses that covered half of her face.

"You just ate one a week ago, you liar," replied the tallest one with a snarky tone. She held an air of authority among this throng of females. She must be the leader.

"Don't be mean, Cindy. You know what I mean. I'm craving it."

"It does smell delicious..." a softer feminine

voice chimed in. This one was partially hidden behind the other two.

"Why do you want to eat this crap if your parents own a restaurant, Kimmy? You should be eating everyday over there, *for free*," the one with the attitude barks out like a command. Her voice grated my nerves and my fingers itched to do something I probably shouldn't do according to human customs and laws.

She wouldn't be this snarky when her soul was tortured down below. The demons of the underworld would make sure of it. I began daydreaming about home and peeling flesh from bone when she casted her gaze in my direction. Her eyes perused my form from the top of my head, downward.

It made my skin crawl.

Here in the human realm, I was forced to take on an appearance that wouldn't disturb the order of things. Though my demon form was perfectly sound, the master didn't want me wreaking havoc up here the same way I did back in the underworld. I scowled at the thought. Wasn't that the best part about being a demon? As part of my punishment, I was forced to 'play nice' while I served my time— and I had to do it looking like one of the locals.

I chose the flesh suit of a muscular male of a taller human build who decorated his body with imagery that kept many humans at bay. Some of the images reminded me of home. In my annoyance at the time of my punishment, I chose to replicate one of the human criminals I had come across back in the underworld—minus his hideous face.

It was my bad luck that human females were irrationally attracted to dark haired men with tattoos. Just like the leader of this little mishmash of females here. I glared at her while she continued to size me up. Her blond roots revealed her true colors but she knew that.

As she tilted her head, I've concluded that females tend to tie their manes to the side in order to make themselves look bigger with their frizzy locks. An attempt at dominance.

The more I looked at her and the rest of them, the more I realized this gaggle of girls weren't girls at all, but older than I initially assumed. I scrutinized the timid one that finally chose to emerge from behind her guardians. She looked younger than the other two and I wondered if she was a wayward straggler they picked up to mother.

"Maybe we should stop for a snack before we hit the streets," the blond one purred before bringing herself to the counter and leaning against it, trying to showcase her upper assets in my direction. Human men would find her attractive from what I had come to learn.

Me? I wanted to gauge her eyes out to see if I could fix her face into something worth giving attention to.

I ignored her and stared at the other two. The shortest of the bunch was the female with the timid voice. She had her dark hair pulled back in a neat ponytail, her hands clasped before her primly as she gazed up at the menu, oblivious to the wretched humans around her.

She had an air of innocence and my perchance for corruption gnawed at me the longer I looked at her. Her blatant lack of overpowering, frizzy mane done two sizes too big for her head only reiterated her submissive nature. How this one got stuck with the other two was beyond my comprehension. She didn't even dress like them. In fact, she was the total opposite without any bright blue war paint splattered across her eyes like the others.

Fingers snapping stole my attention as I slowly turned my head to look at the annoying woman at the counter.

"Hey! I've been calling you twice now. I want an order of number three with a side of fries and the pink lemonade," she barked out.

Without a word, I flicked my gaze at her once and completed her order in silence, continuing to eavesdrop on their conversation. This corner of the Hellscape Mall had nothing else going for it besides the insignificant chatters—part of my punishment, I was sure.

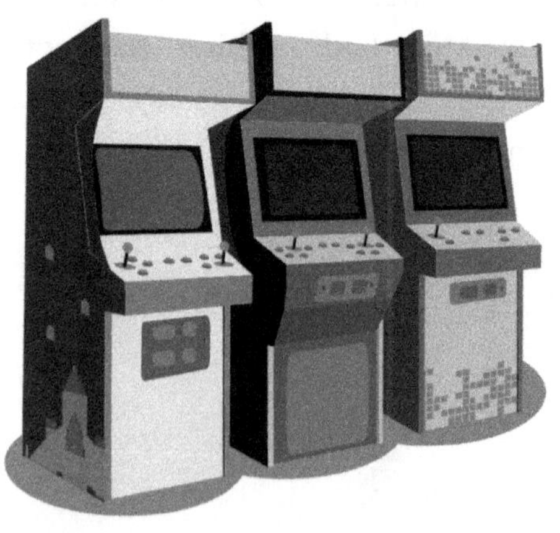

CHAPTER 2

KIMMY

WE'D BEEN WANDERING AROUND THE MALL FOR OVER AN hour at Cindy's insistence. Halloween was coming up and she wanted to find the perfect costume for one of the parties she had lined up. I didn't mind being dragged along with her and Nicole but sometimes their explosive personalities could be exhausting.

But I loved hanging out with them anyway.

It was the perfect place to find what she needed. The hot pink neon sign on the outside was more than inviting and the fact that the building offered much needed air conditioning from the blistering sun also helped. Having grown up most of my life in the desert of Nevada here in Death Canyon City, the halloween decorations along the store fronts in Hellscape Mall only added to the spooky atmosphere. The city itself already had weird legends going on for them, so this was the icing on the metaphorical cake. The more we walked, the more excited I became over all the spiders and ghost and stringy webs.

We'd just finished hitting the upper level stores and decided to come downstairs to the food court for a short snack break. It was located right smack in the middle with all the best eateries. One of the food shops even looked like it was under construction. I was curious to see what was going to pop up there.

Cindy pointed us in the direction of The Good Char and my stomach cramped from both excitement and hunger. I haven't had one of these since I was a teenager. The man working behind the booth was tall, dark and broody with his tattooed arms crossed as we approached. But I was caught by the expanse of the menu and the very delicious looking lemonade dispenser that was in front of me. It was a nice change from the hot teas my mother loved to drink and make for us at home. I should definitely get some lemonade.

Cindy was rambling beside me, as I continued to check out the menu with scrutiny. Wow, there sure were a lot of options for what could be done to a hotdog. This was so fascinating.

"Do you see him?" Cindy snapped, tapping my chest with the backside of her hand with annoyance, stealing my attention. "It's like he is totally ignoring us. Rude."

I inwardly winced, feeling her words were

directed at me as well before looking over at the tall man behind the counter. My eyes widened when I realized he was staring straight at me. I quickly averted my eyes and went back to pursuing the menu while biting my bottom lip out of a nervous habit, mentally cataloging what I wanted.

Cindy did what she always did when she couldn't get her way. She began to snap her fingers in front of the worker. I had to remind myself that our cultures were vastly different and I needed to not mentally judge her.

But if she had a mother like mine, she would have probably been pulled away by her ear by now.

"Hey! I've been calling you twice now. I want an order of number three with a side of fries and the pink lemonade," she called out with her hand on her hip.

I was in awe of her audacity. Cindy was one of pretty girls with her hair beautifully teased before she left the house.

I obediently lined up behind her ready with my order, excitedly with my hands clasped in front of me.

"Three corndogs and three lemonades, you got that?" Cindy ordered again with emphasis.

Oh! How nice, she ordered for us! Without a doubt, the smell that came from this food stall was exquisite. I was drooling over imagining myself taking a huge bite out of the corndog when my attention was drawn to a small sign at the window.

I blinked a few times, slack jawed. It was the answer to one of my prayers and something I needed horribly.

I stared at it again, making sure I wasn't seeing things. But I wasn't. In big, bold black letters, HELP WANTED, stared right back at me.

"Holy cow! Look Cindy!" I pointed to the sign while dancing to the beat in my own head. This was it! I was asking for a sign the other night and here it was!

Cindy immediately snarked at my excitement and I felt myself deflate a little.

"Like, girl, there's no way I would be caught dead working here. The guys will think you are a total spaz. I would rather work with my parents than a place like *this*."

I couldn't be mad at her. It was because she would never understand the things I went through. She was rich and her parents were more than well off. She never had to worry about anything.

I bit my bottom lip as thoughts continued to race through my head. This might just be my way out of the house, which was a total drag since I graduated. My parents weren't terrible, they just weren't what normal parents usually were. They came to this country with a purpose, to make a better life for their family. But their rules and expectations became a bit much the older I became, especially after moving out to Death Canyon City when it first began to populate.

My parents were more than willing to give me the money I needed, but it always came with a cost. So, the perfect solution would be for me to make my own cash quickly. I also needed some type of escape from their helicoptering tendencies.

The broody man behind the counter was quiet as he expertly worked his machines and procedures. I watched with rapt fascination at the way he smoothly operated everything with practiced ease.

When he brought our orders to the counter, he shoved them toward us with a grunt. I tried to contain my giggle of nervousness when I slowly walked up to help grab our orders while Cindy paid. I flicked my gaze to the man, trying to see what his name was but when his eyes shot to mine, I ran away like a coward. Looking around the food court, Nicole had saved us a spot at one of the nearby tables. With a bright smile, I made my way toward her as she got to her feet to help me with the tray.

Once I placed our food down, I stood there awkwardly warring within myself. This was my chance wasn't it? The sign I prayed for when my parents were being overly annoying about my aspirations and when I was going to help manage the family restaurant.

Come on, Kimmy. You are an adult. You can do this!

What if they get mad?

You can't think about that now. This opportunity

might pass you by and then you'll live with regrets and what ifs!

Okay, brain. You're right. I can do this.

I worked up my nerves, turned and took a confident step toward The Good Char so I could inquire about the job.

"Can you, like, hurry up?" Cindy called out, completely annoyed at my detour from our snack break. "This is such a drag. I'm ready to eat," she whined.

I snickered a little, feeling a little lighter in my step. Admittedly, this was Cindy's way of saying she wouldn't hold me back from what I wanted and that gave me the extra confidence I needed to go through with it.

My eyes widened as I took in the owner once again. He stood so large and looming, but he seemed nice. With my hands clasped in front of me to keep my nerves at bay, I stopped right in front of the counter and took a deep breath. I did take notice that he wasn't brooding this time around. That was a good sign, right?

Flutters of butterfly wings in my stomach made me a little lightheaded as I wrung my hands before me, right before I blurted out the question without thinking.

"Has that position been filled, s-sir?" I pointed at the sign and gave him the biggest smile I could, hoping it would convince him to hire me. I had been told I had a friendly face. Places liked that didn't they? It would help drive more customers here, my logical mind supplied me.

I was sweating bullets as he took a few moments to look me over. I knew I was small in comparison to the average American girl. It didn't give much a way as to how hard of a worker I was. I stood there nervously as a few different emotions crossed his features but I continued to smile with hope.

I flicked my eyes to his name tag a few times but the way his large arms crossed, it skewed the angle of it.

Finally, he shook his head and answered with a deep tenor that made my eyes bug out in surprise. "Not yet. The last person who worked for me didn't work out. It's like he fell off the face of the earth."

Perfect! I'll take it! Pick me! Oh, please pick me! Why did he say that last statement slower than the others, though? How very strange.

I cleared my throat and tried to stave off the waiver in my voice. "Well, if you want someone that will give you 110%, I will gladly take the job," I confidently told him.

I had always been a hard worker, my parents raised me that way. Initially, it was a fact that left a slight sour taste in my mouth when talking about it, but now I knew that this would help catapult me where I wanted to go.

"I may be small, but I work super hard and I promise that you won't regret hiring me."

I forced my hands to my side and bit my

bottom lip to stop myself from smiling like a crazed animatronic clown.

"We will see," he said with a scowl pointed in Cindy's direction. I looked over my shoulder in confusion to find Cindy scowling right back. She then rolled her eyes and I could mentally hear her say, "ugh."

"Oh, don't pay any attention to her, she always looks like that," I nervously laughed, hoping he wouldn't change his mind about hiring me. We had such different personalities that I always questioned the saying of birds being similar flocking together.

"If she always looks like that, as you say, she needs to get her face checked out." He turned his attention back on me and I gave him another bright smile. His expression didn't change. "You be here early tomorrow morning and we'll get you trained. The job is yours."

CHAPTER 3

Despite seeing me walk over there, knowing what my purpose was, Cindy was flustered upon my return, crossing her arms with an audible exhale.

"I can't believe you just did that," she huffed before stuffing her face with a corndog.

"You know I've been trying to find a way to not work at the restaurant anymore, Cin! I mentioned it to you, remember?" I sheepishly whined. I wasn't a complainer and I didn't like the feeling I got from having to explain it to her again.

"But a hotdog shop? Really?"

Nicole quietly ate her corndog as she stared over both our shoulders. I was too excited to be as bothered as Cindy wanted me to be. There were so many things that I could do with this extra money and there was nothing she could do or say that would take my excitement away.

Taking a bite out of my corndog, my stomach purred in satisfaction. I happily turned around and waved at my new boss before taking another bite. We devoured our amazing food and drank down our pink lemonade with a giant gulp. Cindy and Nicole finished up their meals and quickly got up to throw away their paper trays.

I took one last delicious bite and waved at my new boss once more before tossing my food away but kept my drink. He stared at me with a blank expression but I knew he was excited to have me on board as well.

"So where are we going next?" Nicole asked.

"I don't know but I have loads of energy now that my stomach is full!" I giddily answered before taking another sip. The cold liquid was refreshing and gave me a pep to my step.

We continued to explore the stores on the bottom level and I couldn't take my mind off the fact that with my new job, soon I would be able to do all the things I wanted to do.

"Girl, what you need to do is party more," Cindy called out to me from across one of the clothing racks. "Greg took me to Deadman's Hill last night, and girl, he pulled out his little dick and asked me to suck it. I told him I wasn't interested in cocktail weiners," she laughed.

I choked on the remnants of ice in my cup, spitting it everywhere. Feeling flush from embarrassment, I quickly wiped my mouth with the back of my hand, hoping no one saw me.

"That is so funny. I mean, how uncool can someone be? Like, eww, but you really need to calm down," Nicole told her with nonchalance. "You are going out with a new guy every week and I mean, are you sleeping with them?"

Cindy gave us a sly smile before tapping finger at the corner of her mouth in consideration. "Well, only if they have a nice large—"

"Okay!" I exclaimed, tossing the rest of my drink away in a nearby trash can loudly. "I don't want to know!" I placed my hands over my ears and began humming.

She was my best friend and I know I'm not supposed to judge her but she was becoming a tramp and didn't realize it. Cindy needed to understand that she was so much more than what her body had to offer.

Nicole bursted out with a laugh and they both turned into a fit of timed giggles by the end of it. I rolled my eyes and gave them a smile, unable to help myself. It was contagious.

We exited the clothing store after Cindy bought some sexy lingerie and looked left and right. The Pizzeria Arcade enticed everyone nearby with animatronic laughter and a bustle of teenagers constantly streaming inside. All of the stores lined up near us offered everything a person could want. It was no wonder teenagers loved to hang out here, getting lost for hours on end.

"Where should we go next?" I asked the girls, my eyes straying to the Dark Spells Comic shop.

"Girlfriend! Is that you?"

We all turned to see several people coming toward us, none that I recognized. They must be

Cindy's other friends from her subdivision from the looks of them. I stood there silently as they began chatting up.

"I see you brought your pet with you," a tall red headed girl, dressed in a fashionable checkered dress and high top sneakers noted. The other two girls giggled at her joke, which I didn't understand, when Cindy quickly put them in their place.

"Pet?" she snapped. "She's my friend and a hell of a better friend than you! So if you don't like her, see yourself the hell away from us. You got that?"

She grabbed my arm and pulled me right between them, splitting the crowd like the red sea. Most of their mouths hung open, some of them glaring but I innocently turned my head away and continued to let Cindy lead me from the wolves with Nicole following right behind us.

I didn't know what happened, but I also didn't like the vibe I got from them by the way they looked at me. I hope Cindy wasn't mad because of me being awkward around them.

"Let's go. We don't have time to talk to losers, Kimmy," she said aloud for them to hear even though we were already a few feet away. "They let anyone in here, don't they?"

I blinked a few times. Was she mad at them and not at me?

She began to giggle and then Nicole joined in over her crazy antics. I pretended to laugh boisterously with her but that red headed girl really did hurt my feelings now that I knew she was talking about me. I get it. I wasn't the prettiest and I didn't look like them with my obvious straight black hair. I didn't have the money they have.

Maybe Cindy would be better off without me. *She should be hanging out with people like them, shouldn't she? Instead of keeping a sore thumb like me around because she was being nice.*

As if reading my change in mood, Cindy quickly piped up again. "Girl, you know what would cheer you up? Photo booth! Let's take some bestie pictures!" she squealed. Her enthusiasm made me smile because sometimes I didn't feel I deserved such a good friend.

She dragged both Nicole and I across a few stores until we spotted one. We all climbed inside the picture booth together and began making funny poses, holding up peace signs and making a lot of other bizarre moves while the camera flashed. Once it was done, we spilled out of the booth in a fit of giggles as we impatiently waited for the pictures to print.

We hugged each other while the pics finally decided to print out. They looked so cool. I pulled out my trusty scissors from my purse and began to cut each picture individually.

"Smart, Kimmy!" Cindy crowed. "Who knew your nerdiness with sewing would come in handy, eh?"

"Man, I want this one!" Nicole pointed out and I eagerly tried to cut faster.

We decided which pics we each wanted before

we walked arm in arm into the gameroom in bright moods.

The gameroom was where every teen wanted to be, from basketball, to fighting games, bowling and games of skill. This place was the coolest. The flashing lights and all the people winning prizes made it a place of pure relaxation in the midst of total chaos. Despite our ages, we still found this to be the best place to unwind.

"Ms. Pacman!" Cindy yelled in excitement before hurrying to put money into the token machine. "You are going down this time, I promise you that, little Miss high score."

"You sure about that?" Nicole laughed, flicking her gaze at me knowingly, before she wandered off to play something solo.

I waved at her, knowing we'd meet back up later as I followed behind Cindy. When I got to the machine, Cindy placed her token in and, like always, the highest score came on the screen and there was my name at the very top: **gamerqueen.**

"Yeah, just you watch me take that high score from you," she taunted. Cindy was always so competitive with me. Some might see it as one of her flaws, I saw it as one of her endearing qualities. I laughed off her threat because when it came to games, she was pretty bad. But I let her think I was scared she could beat me. It was what best friends did.

One minute in and Cindy was leaning toward the machine. I stood there calmly, making my moves in silence as a few other patrons stopped to watch us.

"I'm coming for you, Kimmy! Eat your heart out!"

"Okay, Cindy," I replied with a soft smile.

Her excitement crashed and burned after losing several thousands of points from my high score. I covered my mouth trying to hide my laughter because Cindy was the world's biggest sore loser.

"Ugh! This thing is broken!" she growled, giving it a little kick before standing there with her hands balled into fists, fuming. I was surprised steam wasn't coming out of her ears or perhaps it did and that was why the small crowd around us began dispersing quickly.

"It probably is," I teased. "Hey, let's go play skee-ball instead!"

Her frown turned into a sparkling in her eye as she pivoted and fast walked toward the next game against me. It was moments like these that my confidence was strong. Cindy had a way of making me put down my walls when I was around her. We went way back to the beginning of Death Canyon City.

Nicole joined our dynamic duo not long ago so I was still feeling her out. Cindy vouched for her though, mentioning that things at home for her weren't the best. I could understand that and empathized with her.

"You're going down, Cin!" I laughed and with

her index finger and thumb, she placed an L on her forehead, mouthing that I was going down first. We both got serious as the game started.

Thirty minutes in and I easily beat her again, gaining hundreds of tickets. I did a little dance as Cindy stomped her feet and turned her face away. She was so funny.

I grabbed all the tickets in my arms and made my way toward her. "Come on, Cin! Let's see what we can get with these!"

Her frown turned upside down and we both laughed as we walked up to the counter to cash them in for several cheap novelty items.

"Why did you get more than me?" Cindy whined as she stuck her thumbs in her ears, wiggling her fingers and sticking her tongue out like the immature brat she was.

"Stop being a brat, Cin," I playfully teased, slapping her arm.

"Someone's gotta take the spot. Might as well be me!" she singsonged.

"Woah! Nice pot guys!" came Nicole's voice, her hands full of her own small prizes.

"Right?" I asked, throwing my arm over Cindy's shoulder and pulling her in against me. "It was great teamwork."

Nicole rolled her eyes but said nothing as we both made our way out of the gameroom.

"Hey guys, I need to check one more store, but you don't have to come with me. I'll see you guys tomorrow or something? Call me," she mimed a phone with her hand—thumb pointing toward her ear, the other finger acting as the receiver end.

We nodded and waved at her, watching her walk away from us. Shrugging my shoulders, Cindy looped her arm in mine and we both headed out the front glass doors of the mall. The moment the doors opened, the heat blasted our faces and we both groaned in unison.

I playfully shoved her off me, the leather of her jacket starting to stick to my skin. We both laughed when a small pickup with a rollbar pulled up with several guys inside. They rolled down their window and called in our direction—well, in Cindy's direction.

"Hey sexy, wanna come and sit on my lap," the guy from the passenger seat suggested.

I cringed but Cindy responded smoothly the way she always did. "How much booze ya got?"

Was she kidding? Booze, in this heat? We served booze at the family restaurant, but I was never tempted to try. Yellow liquids looked wrong to me.

The guy lifted up a twelve pack and Cindy laughed, looking at him seductively. "Sure, I will come with you Jarred."

She knew him? I mean, it didn't matter, look at them! Look at what they were suggesting! I quickly grabbed her wrist.

"They've already been drinking. You don't need to be riding with them to god knows where Cin, you need to grow up and think," I pleaded.

"Grow up?" she snapped, automatically turning defensive. "Really? You are the one with a bottle stuck up your ass! I am grown and I will go with whoever the hell I want to go with, now let me go!"

She jerked her arm back and I was hurt. Couldn't she see that I cared about her?

"Fine! Then go!" I said in a huff, turning my heel in frustration as I walked away from them all. The truck sped past me with a roar of the engine, their laughter fading away into the distance while the truck accelerated up the street.

I wasn't going to let it bother me, not one bit. *I hope she gets so drunk that her hangover tomorrow makes her sick all day.*

Once the thought left my mind, guilt assaulted me and my eyes burned with unshed tears. After walking about thirty minutes in the blazing heat, I made it home and ran up the stairs and closed my door. I threw my purse on the floor and fell face first across my bed, replaying the argument Cindy over and over in my head until I fell asleep.

CHAPTER 4

The next morning came fast. It felt like I only closed my eyes for ten minutes. I jumped out of bed quickly, put on my pants and a tie-dyed t-shirt and swiftly ran down the stairs and outside to my bicycle.

"Oh, no. My helmet!" I jumped off, ran back into the house. When I returned outside, I quickly picked the bicycle up and headed to The Good Char.

He told me to come today. I needed to make sure I was there early.

I rode my bike as fast as I could on the sidewalk while enjoying the breeze of the cooler morning air and ringing my bell so I wouldn't accidentally run over anyone. The sun was already starting to rise higher as I parked my bicycle and made my way into the front of the mall. The doors were already unlocked for the other employees and a security guard sat at the front, nodding to me in greeting. I waved and used quick strides toward the food court. I arrived to find the manager already sweeping the floor and grumbling to himself.

I guess his broody personality really was just deeply rooted and not because of people around him.

"Darn kids with no training, how hard is it to put trash in the garbage can?" he griped. I watched nervously as he cleaned in front of his area, bending over to pick up cups and tossing it in the nearby trash bin. His biceps stretched the sleeve of his black shirt as he grabbed his broom again.

I felt bad. I should be the one doing that. Teenagers didn't care about keeping our environment clean, it was something that frustrated me too. I walked over to where he was cleaning and without speaking a word, began to pick up the trash with him.

"You're the girl I hired yesterday," he snarled while shaking his head at the last bit of trash on the floor.

"Yes, I am. I'm so sorry, I didn't catch your name the other day. My name is Kimmy," I told him cheerfully.

He looked at me like he was constipated and I worried if he was taking care of himself. Maybe that was why he needed extra help at The Good Char.

"Dzik. Call me Dzik."

Huh. Haven't heard that one before. But what do I know?

I beamed and quickly went to grab the broom from his hands to alleviate him of the mundane tasks. As the manager, he shouldn't have to do this. He was so kind in taking me in as an employee. I wanted to show him my gratitude.

While I swept, I began to nervously ramble, trying to get my bearings around him. "I figured I should come and get an early start on learning everything I could from you about my job. I mean, sweeping is sweeping no matter where you are, but the stuff behind the counter, that's something else."

Thank goodness there wasn't a lot of trash left. I quickly finished cleaning around our area and then gave him a brilliant smile when I was done.

Mr. Dzik was decked in all black beneath his apron. Despite being in shorts, he looked good, like he couldn't be anything other than a manager of something here. I looked at myself and my face flushed with embarrassment.

"Oh, was I supposed to get a uniform? I'm so sorry. That was my fault. I should have asked for one the other day. Do you by any chance have any on hand that would fit me?" I gave him my best puppy dog eyes and realized that beyond his grumpy exterior, he wasn't that much older than me—I didn't think. He looked to be in his mid thirties, possibly.

That constipated look was back.

He shook his head and stared at me with such intensity that my face flamed even more. I tended to ramble when I was nervous and feeling like I was letting someone down. I didn't want to let him down on my first day.

After we both finished, he mumbled something and walked behind the counter into a back room. He wasn't gone long before reappearing with an apron draped across his arm. He threw it at me and I almost didn't catch it in time if it wasn't for my awkward acrobatics saving me before I could fall. I turned them in my hands and examined them with pride. *The Good Char* was written across the chest.

"What was your name again?" he grunted. "I have to make a name tag for you."

I beamed at him and quickly put my apron on. "It's Kimmy, Mr. Dzik."

My first real job that didn't require me working for my parents. This new experience was totally exciting for me. A woman of the world without any ties to the Ngo name. I wasn't ashamed of my name, but I needed to do something for myself without obligation and expectation hanging over my head.

I quickly finished another round of sweeps right outside our area before following him behind the counter. Gently leaning the broom to lean against the wall, I clasped my hands in front of me and watched everything he did closely.

When he began turning things on and setting things up, I got on my tiptoes and leaned around his wide body to get a good look. I was distracted by how veiny his forearms were. I didn't realize my breathing was picking up when he sputtered and quickly turned to look down at me with a frown.

"What are you doing?" he barked.

I smiled. "Learning!"

"Have you never worked before, girl?"

Uh oh. That constipated look was back. I straightened and squared my shoulders before looking at him innocently. I didn't want him to think I was incompetent. I really wanted this job to work out.

"Y-yes, sir, I have. But mostly in my parents' restaurant. I've tried my hand with the wok a time or two but almost burned my hair off so they placed me elsewhere. The back office with my parents is kind of boring, so occasionally I help on the floor. I've never worked with corndogs before. We don't serve corndogs at the restaurant. Sir. I mean, Mr. Dzik."

"Dzik. Just Dzik." He looked at me curiously and I tried my best to not be a bother. "You're going to man the register for now. Get familiar with the names on the menu and the prices. We'll go from there."

"Yes, sir!" I saluted him and quickly positioned myself where I needed to be, taking my assignment seriously. "Oh! I didn't know we had a breakfast menu! People actually eat corndogs for breakfast?"

"You are a peculiar human," he grumbled as he casted his gaze in my direction before bringing out the secret batter. I mean, it must be a secret because he doesn't want me over there yet. Maybe one day he'll tell me what it was made of and I would finally understand why his corndogs are so addictive.

The first customer made his way in our direction and my excitement spiked to epic proportions. I straightened my back and waved happily only to find the elderly man continue walking past us and around the rest of the food court in a loop. *Oh.*

A chuckle came from behind me and I quickly turned to find Mr. Dzik—I mean, Dzik snickering.

I joined in. "That was kind of funny, wasn't it? I totally thought he was a customer."

Dzik shook his head as he watched the hotdogs burn on the grill that was constantly rotating. "A lot of the ancient ones come to Hellscape Mall to get their exercise in. They don't have any interest in eating. It's probably what preserves them."

Some of the things he said were so funny.

"How nice! I should encourage my parents to do that too. Wait, ancient? You're so silly Dzik. They're not that old. That man that passed us couldn't be older than sixty. If they're ancient, what does that make you?" I teased.

He curled his lip into an adorable snarl and huffed, crossing his arms over his chest. I was distracted by the intricate images and flames that slithered and wrapped around his forearm when his voice pulled me back to attention.

"It makes me your damn boss. Now get back to work!" he barked.

I squealed at his sudden change in demeanor

and quickly turned around and faced the heart of the mall with my heart pounding inside of my chest.

Was it wrong of me to say that it still made me excited to see what the day would bring?

CHAPTER 5

DZIK

THIS BIZARRE HUMAN GIRL HAD THE STRANGEST reactions to things around her. Her overly jovial nature disgusted me but she seemed like she was willing to do my bidding and that was all I needed for this wretched shop. I needed to be able to remove myself from the humans when my aggravation got the better of me.

I stared at Kimmy's back curiously. It looked like she was trying her best to stop herself from dancing to a tune only she could hear. Strange. What was she so happy about? The only people milling around Hellscape Mall at this hour were humans that needed to let go of their tight grip on life.

But unlike my last employee, she didn't look like she minded working.

"Kimmy!" I growled. Caught in my thoughts, I

almost missed her inching her way toward the grill. "Stay away from that grill."

I made my way over to her in two strides, picked her up and plopped her back behind the register. I was going to have to watch out for this one. She was wiley, like that cartoon coyote those annoying little human minions liked to watch on television.

Kids, my mind supplied me. Humans called their spawn kids. Why they wished to name them after goat offspring was beyond me.

I didn't need the master getting on me about another wayward soul finding its way in places it didn't belong. I looked at Kimmy again who waved animatedly at another ancient human walking by. I wouldn't hear the last of it if she fell into the vortex. Her soul was too innocent and pure.

"Are you guys open?" a new voice approached us. It was the old man who passed her the first time.

"Yes!" she squeaked with excitement. "What can I get you?"

He rambled off his order and her fingers flew nimbly across the register. When she looked over her shoulder in my direction with a smile, I cleared my throat and turned away to complete his order before handing it to her.

"There you go! Enjoy your meal!" she hollered after him after he left, almost falling over the counter with how far she was leaning.

"Get your feet back on the ground!" I growled,

grabbing the back of her shirt and pulling her back into place. "You don't need to glue yourself to the customers once they're gone. Just place their orders."

She bounced on her feet as she turned to me. "Did I do good? He looked happy! First satisfied customer of the day!"

When she clapped her little hands in front of her, I ran my hand down my face. What had I gotten myself into?

I grumbled and walked away, leaving her in her happy little bubble as I observed the mall picking up over the course of the next hour.

Kimmy excitedly greeted anyone within a ten foot radius and I had to physically pull her back a few more times before my command to keep her feet on the ground went through her thick skull. I was finally at my wits end when I stomped to the back room, came back and slammed a stool down in front of the register, glaring at her while pointing at it.

To my vexation she did her little clap and hopped on, crossing her legs, diligently looking out for more customers as if she was on a mission.

Working The Good Char in the realm of men was the worst punishment the master could bestow upon me. For all I knew, he probably planted Kimmy here just to watch me suffer. I peered at her through the side of my eye and wondered if the master would shorten my sentence if I tainted her soul. It would show him that I deserved my old position back.

"Mr. Dzik, what else can I do now?" she asked with enthusiasm, following me around the area like one of Sabnock's nasty rashes. "Are you going to show me how to do the corndogs?"

"No."

"Pretty, please! I'm a fast learner, I promise! I just want to make your day easier. That's what I'm here for."

Was she? I was suddenly sure she was here to torment me with her monstrously happy demeanor.

"Take a seat somewhere if there are no customers," I commanded.

"But what if they don't see me? I'm not that tall. It's the Asian in me. They might think we're closed. It's okay. Thank you though. I'll just stand behind the register and wait for the next person to come," she rambled as she hurried back to the counter.

My head hurt as my annoyance climbed—and it wasn't even lunch hour yet. I needed to get her out of my hair before I threw her in the vortex myself.

"Kimmy," I called out.

She popped up like an animated character in one of their human box contraptions and quickly ran back to my side, eyes sparkling. "Yes, Mr. Dzik?"

I leaned back, not wanting whatever infected

her to get on me. When she leaned in with a smile that overtook her face, I grimaced and blurted out the only thing I could think of to get her away from me. "Pop open the fridge and grab a pop. This will be your breaktime for today."

Her eyes practically shone like diamonds as if flames danced within her. It was both fascinating and horrifying.

"Really? Oh wow! My parents never gave me a break. Especially not one this early. And with a treat to boot! Thank you, Mr. Dzik!" she sang at an awkward pitch.

She skipped over to the fridge and I exhaled a sigh of relief. That was close. I bet if she touched me, I'd end up infected with whatever positivity that was inside of her. It couldn't be normal. Something was definitely wrong with this little human. But that wasn't my problem. I just needed her to work The Good Char.

With her finally occupied, I began creating more batter. The lull in customers and quiet eased me as I rhythmically mixed and stirred. Suddenly, a chill ran down my spine. There were unwanted eyes on me. I slowly looked over my shoulder to find Kimmy's eyes staring intently at everything I was doing with a pen and little notepad.

How the hell did she manage to bring one with her when she didn't even have a purse?

"And just what are you doing?" I asked through gritted teeth, my paranoia rising to infernal levels.

"Why are you writing? And why are you looking at me like that?"

"Well, I was writing down your steps according to what you were doing," she explained, nodding with seriousness. "You can never be too prepared."

She placed the pencil behind her ear and stuffed the writing tablet in front of her apron pocket.

I stood there, contemplating what she said for a few moments. I never had an employee so diligently want to learn before. My lips twitched in a slight smirk. This could work out well for me.

"Why don't you use that writing tablet you have and take down orders as they come. Then hand it to me and I can prepare the food. I cook and you take the money and put it in the money box and give change. You can count, can't you?" I asked after giving some thought to the fact she never told me how old she was.

"Of course, I can count, Mr. Dzik," she giggled, covering her mouth with her dainty little hand.

Why would she think she could stop herself from laughing with her hand that far from her face? The best way for anyone to stop something from coming out of a human mouth would be to slap their hand entirely over their face and shove them into the flames—

"I graduated highschool five years ago and I have just been working for my parents," she continued while going over to sit down on the stool. "But sometimes you need to make a life for yourself, ya know? Not for my Mom or Dad, but me."

I looked at her, perplexed. How in the world did the conversation route itself in this direction?

"I really didn't need to know all of that. The only thing I needed to know is if you could count." These humans were too much. It was a wonder they managed to stay alive this long. You ask them one simple question and they will tell you their entire life story. "You better enjoy that break of yours. It's nearly lunchtime and we're about to get swamped. Today, we'll see how much you really want your job."

"Oh, yes, Mr. Dzik," she replied obediently, straightening her back, her face showing nothing but pure determination. My eyes flicked below her face involuntarily for a second and then back. All this positivity was causing me to itch. I wanted to scour my skin in acid and peel it from the overload of her upbeat attitude. It was humans like her that were causing a shortage of souls back home in the underworld.

Right on cue, I could hear the crowd begin to gather as the mall became alive with chatter. I could feel a line begin to form in front of the counter. The presence of a human crowd always made my skin prickle with the need to torture something.

I looked over to her with a wicked grin. "It's showtime, Kimmy. Take your time and it will be fine."

I wanted to break her, show her that working under me wasn't going to be as easy as she thought.

As if possessed, she stood up with a fire in her eyes, wrapped her hair into a bun and walked over to the front counter like she owned the place. With her pad in hand she leaned over the counter with a large smile and was bombarded immediately by the first customer.

She happily took orders with giggles in a meticulous manner, handing me the notes and quickly taking the next order. I stood there dumbfounded as I watched her, running the register like a pro.

Where the hell did she learn to handle orders like this? She acted like she never had a job before despite her ramblings about whatever it was the humans that birthed her did.

There was definitely more to this girl than meets the eye.

"Mr. Dzik, we need to push!" she called out boldly. "We got a bigger crowd coming."

She walked back and grabbed the first couple of completed orders and calculated the change before handing them their food—all the while humming cheerily as if she was in her element.

To my dismay and wonderment, my business had never run this smoothly before and it was only her first day. I could get used to this. Other than all of that humming and smiling, she was actually... okay.

I narrowed my eyes. This may work out after all. I was one of the smartest demons there was! And the master needed to see that for himself.

I nodded to myself at my own brilliance.

I had been in the human realm long enough. It should be time for me to come home!

CHAPTER 6

We worked tirelessly together in perfect unison. And after a few horrid hours, it finally slowed down. I took a seat on one of my folding chairs and so did she on her little stool that was much too tall for her short legs.

"Phew! That was quite a rush, wasn't it, Mr. Dzik?" she pretended to wipe her brow but I saw no perspiration. What was she playing at? "But we got everything done," she prattled on with a bubbly expression.

And there goes the hives again. This girl was either going to be the death of me... or make me rich in the realm of men.

After sitting for what felt like less than a minute, she hopped up, walked to the fridge, quickly came back and handed me a soda. Time stood suspiciously still as I stared at the water drop on the outside slowly sliding down. I should let it hit the floor and watch her slip to her death, but instead I hesitantly took the syrupy can of liquid and observed as she drank one in inhuman gulps while walking herself back over to the counter.

She began to clean all of the trash, then placed the trays on the counter and ran hot dishwater in the sink.

The little menace wouldn't stop moving long enough for me to figure out what she was up to. Slamming my can on the counter furiously, I stood up and glared at her.

"What are you doing?" I snarled. "I didn't ask you to clean up."

She looked over with a smile that reached her ears and continued to wash the trays without looking at them. "It needs to be done, Mr. Dzik. You go on and rest, this is what you are paying me for."

My head pounded until her words made a light go off in my head. I slowly sat back down without taking my eyes off her back, watching the wayward tendrils of her hair sway, threatening to get plastered to the back of her neck.

So this human was willing to be a servant to me? I had been looking at this hiring help thing all wrong.

My lips twitched.

Now, *I* was the master and *she* was the servant, eh? Perhaps she wasn't planted here for my torture after all. The more I thought about it, the more I grinned.

Nodding my head, I leaned back, putting my

feet up on the side of the counter while I watched her clean, tidy all the paper trays meticulously and rearrange the paper cups in order by size and groups of twenty.

When her little figure moved to turn off the deep frying in an attempt to empty it, I shot to my feet as if the master himself was on my hide.

"Okay, that's it!" I pointed at her and gritted my teeth while stomping over to her. I leaned into her face until I smashed my nose against hers. "Where did you work before you came here? You know a little too much about the cooking business to be a rookie."

I inwardly admitted I was completely blown away at her knowledge and speed. But at the same time, my paranoia began to creep in again, telling me this was too good to be true.

"Well...," she started with suspicious awkward laughter that didn't reflect anything funny having happened. I jerked back when she straightened from her initial cowering position to a bold woman with one finger pointing upward. What was this? "I'm so glad you asked, Mr. Dzik! It's so nice of you to want to get to know your employees more. You see—"

What? "That wasn't—"

She cleared her throat and continued before I could complete my thought. "My last name is Ngo, as I mentioned. You know, the giant Ngo diner?" She maniacally laughed to herself and placed her hand on her stomach. My eyes zoomed in as if she casted a spell on me. Grinding my teeth together, I shook my head and glared at her face.

"Sorry, it's always funny to hear it out loud. It kind of rhymed! Well, maybe not. But close enough. Anyway, it's owned and operated by my parents. I've worked there since I was thirteen, right?" she said triumphantly and I took a step back, wondering if all this blabbering was a lie.

She doesn't look that much older.

She placed her finger under her chin, deep in thought before she began prattling on once more with enthusiasm. "No! I was eleven when I started waiting tables. I was thirteen when I started helping in the kitchen. Either way, I have worked in restaurants most of my life," she shrugged as if this was all normal for the typical human female.

I absorbed everything she was spilling about herself. Even I, being a demon, had heard of that diner. Strange that their daughter had been uncorrupted by money and power. *It still didn't explain why she chose to work here.* I decided to keep my thoughts to myself for the time being, until I was able to collect more information.

"That's enough for the day, Kimmy. Be here at the same time tomorrow," I instructed, before mumbling, "You did good."

She literally preened and glowed at the praise. I filed this information away in the back of my head.

"Thank you, Mr. Dzik! I promise I will make you proud." When she smiled brightly this time, a hint of a dimple appeared on her left cheek, stealing my focus. I cleared my throat and watched as she danced and took off her apron, folded it expertly then quickly turned to leave the area and skipped toward the mall's exit.

I blinked a few times, wondering what in the blazes just happened.

It wasn't yet time for the place to close but I didn't care. I followed a few feet behind her, wanting to know how she brought herself here.

"Hey! I want a corndog!" someone hollered. My back stiffened and I looked over my shoulder and gave the ingrate a vicious snarl. The teenage boy squealed like swine and slipped as he tried to jump back, crawling backward until he turned and ran away. The other customers who were beginning to line up at the shop slowly backed away and followed his example.

Ignoring them all, I made long strides to the front of the mall to watch Kimmy pedal herself away on a light blue bicycle across the parking lot with a white, flowery basket in the front. She rang her little bell when someone was but a yard away to warn them of her arrival.

She was a conundrum. She couldn't possibly be from the realm of men. So how exactly did she stumble upon my earthly prison, then? I shook my head and made my way back into the mall without any answers. The sun had gone down some time ago, the other food vendors now slowly closing shop one at a time.

"How's your new employee working out for ya, Dick?"

I growled, turning to find Justin, the manager of the sickly sweet pastry shop from two bays down. He crossed his arms over his midnight blue apron and smirked. Justin was always trying to find a way to steal my customers. As if his customers' sugar crashes brought them back. They didn't. They always ended up venturing toward my counter for our signature lemonade made from the tears of men.

"Better than the two you have. Better get back to your counter, Justin, looks like one of your employees is about to fornicate over the dough."

His face reddened as he quickly turned around and started spitting expletives. The two employees ceased their lip lock and scrambled to get back into positions.

I snickered as Justin continued to lecture them and threaten their jobs.

The crowd dwindled as the night went on. I put everything away, turned off the lights and closed up the shop. Sitting on the stool in the shadows, I waited for the rest of the food court staff to make their way home, watching as their bodies released the tension they had been holding onto during work hours.

Once all of the humans were away sans the security that walked the parameter, it was time for me to open the portal back home. My eyes tracked his movements, making sure he was well out of my line of sight before I made my move.

Turning the knob, the igniter crackled a couple of times before the flames jumped and came alive with the smell of burnt flesh still on the metal. With a wide grin, I felt the hairs on my arm singe right before I contorted myself and jumped into it. Darkness and tortured screams engulfed my short trip as I landed feet first back on familiar grounds. Chitter chatters faded in and out, claws pulling at my flesh suit as I straightened myself to my full height, taking in the desolate landscape and the familiar decaying, sulfuric scent of home.

The roaring flames and dark mountains were a comfort to me as were the screams of agony in the background, constantly playing like a lullaby. *I missed this place.*

"Hey, Dick. I see you're back from the human realm. Still on punishment, eh?" A familiar voice sounded from behind me, making my shoulders tense in agitation.

CHAPTER 7

MY PROBATION DEMON, ZYCHOR, LAUGHED. CHITTER chatters of sprites fading in and out around us added to his disgusting, teasing voice. He was a tall, bony looking creature with curved horns and a grotesque face only a mother could love—except for the fact that he didn't have a mother. I didn't blame the universe one bit. Nothing wanted to claim *that* thing came out of their womb.

"It's Dzik, you fool. You already know I'm here for my normal pick up," I snarled.

His smile grew wider, showcasing rows of sharp fangs. I never did like the bastard. The authority he had over my punishment added to the inflated ego he already sported, expanding his inhuman head into a warped shape.

As if he knew what I was thinking, a long tongue snaked out and flickered in my direction.

My hands itched to rip it out of his skull when better company came toward us with a giant grin.

Belchar was a demon of adultery and one of the few I got along with well.

"You know the master still wants to kill you, right?" he teased.

"I made one little mistake," I grumbled and ran a hand down my face, needing to complete my allotted task before having to return to the realm of men. "A soul escaped under my watch and they were revived somehow, following some of the sprites back to the other side. My bladder threatened to rip me open and I answered its call. It wasn't my fault they escaped, and the master is still charging me with that shit. Plus, I've been in the human realm for one measly soul—and the guy died a week later!"

Crossing my arms, my claws extended and I was tempted to score my flesh suit in agitation when one of the sprites chitter chattered and poofed in front of me, pointing an accusatory finger at my face. I grabbed its neck and kicked it back into the flames licking up the side of one of the mountain walls nearby. The sprite splattered against the surface into black goo, sliding down to the ground before reforming into a cackling being once more.

"Yeah, but he went up above," Belchar needlessly reminded me, pointing his finger upward with a twist of his face. To think that I thought he was on my side. "*That's* why the master's pissed off."

"Right, right," I humored him, glaring in his

direction. He threw his head back and let out a booming laugh, holding his stomach while I continued. "Who would've thought he would do so much good and get to go up *there*." I pointed upward with a disgusted look. "But enough of all this blabbering. My time here is nearly up and I *will* be back home soon enough, doing what I normally do—torturing human souls with the rest of you lot."

"Aren't you torturing them now? I mean you are in the human realm...where all the humans come from?" Belchar questioned with a confused look on his beast-like face. His tusks and half sloughed off skin wrinkled as he gave me another wide grin, holding back his laugh.

"Do you have any idea of the torment I am under?" I gritted out. "Do you even want to know what I'm doing? I'm feeding them, that's what I'm doing. But because I'm a demon and enjoy being evil, I'm feeding them human flesh from the underworld which I then turned into breaded weiners dipped in their own vat of torture."

An awkward pregnant pause passed between us before the two demons in front of me fell over each other laughing, slapping each other's heads like imbeciles.

It really wasn't that funny.

"T-They're eating human flesh?" Zychor snorted.

I began to laugh with them the moment sprites popped onto their shoulders and fell to the ground from cackling in their chitter chatters. I lost my own breath while slapping my knees, the humor in the moment too much to overcome. Humans were fools.

"Yes, well," I slowed down to a chuckle and caught my breath. "It is kind of funny and ironic that humans will pretty much eat fried anything. Especially the ones that come to my counter."

Belchar rolled his eyes once he got a hold of himself. "So, you're feeding humans. That's so *dastardly*, Dzik," he snickered.

When my punishment was over, I was going to rip his arm off and shove it in his gaping maw. "I'll have you know I have done extraordinarily bad things since I've been gone!" I snapped, my tail whipping about angrily having torn through the back of my flesh suit. "I have done *horrible* things since I left, things that would make your skin crawl."

One of the mountains in the distance roared as it erupted, sending volcanic ash into the air for an added dramatic flare to the moment.

"Oh, do tell," piped in Zychor. "Tell us all the bad you've done since you've been in the other realm."

I sputtered and then cleared my throat, my hands on my hips with my chest puffed. "I randomly break parking meters! I have single handedly jaywalked several times and, not to mention, told a police officer a drug deal was going to happen."

All laughter around us ceased before it started anew, aggravatingly louder this time around. My head felt hot from the flush beneath my skin and I bared my teeth at the sprites, grabbing the closest one and throwing it to channel my anger.

"Hey, imbecile," Belchar choked out. "That's a *good* deed. And you breaking the parking meter gave them all the time they needed, it saved them from getting a ticket."

Zychor fell, laughing so hard his horns got lodged in the dry, cracked ground. Sprites began to appear on his chest, dancing and laughing with him like a bunch of monkeys in a human circus.

"And about that jaywalk thing. We heard all about it," Belchar continued. "That guy that swerved around you, missing you after *almost* killing you? He was supposed to have an accident right up the street from where you walked because he was drunk. But instead, he pulled over and fell asleep and no one was harmed. Great job *demoning.*"

Belchar shook his head in utter disappointment and I felt my shoulders slouch as Zychor got back on his feet, dusting himself off and shaking his head in my direction as well.

"Your demon card is about to be pulled," Zychor chortled. "I hear angels are accepting applications."

Leaving the two bastards behind me, I stomped my way into the mountainside, weaving through the tunnels until I came upon the chamber I was looking for.

"Blasted ingrates. I'll show them," I mumbled under my breath.

In the far dark corners, shadows covered most of the crates, filled with products, waiting for me. The master hadn't yet caught wind of my little arrangement with the demon of iniquity. As long as we kept our tight schedule and our mouths shut, he wouldn't ever have to know. He was a busy man after all.

Ignoring the earlier annoyance, I rolled my shoulder and made my way toward them when I caught sight of a familiar face from my periphery.

My former employee, Daniel.

All the souls around us cried out for mercy as Melkgard continued humming a tune, chopping on his table.

"All your shipments should be ready, Dzik," he laughed as he slammed down his blade once more with a loud thud. One of the fingers slipped and rolled onto the floor beside his hind leg, leaving a trail of red.

I nodded in acknowledgement despite him keeping his back to me.

"Dzik!" one of the souls cried out as I performed ergonomically sound human body mechanics before lifting the first crate. I needed to keep chances of injuries down if I was to move all these crates efficiently.

"Dzik!" I looked over my shoulder to see

Daniel, reaching his arm through his cage, his face distorted in anger. "Why didn't you tell me that you were a demon? I was a great employee, wasn't I? How could you let this happen? Let me out of here, please, Mr. Dzik!"

"Silence, human!" I snap, straightening out my knees. "It wasn't my fault that your stupidity led you to fall into the vortex. Now, you'll be trapped here in the underworld forever, especially around the likes of Melkgard. Plus, you were a thief, stealing not only from me but from your dead mother *and* you cheated on your girlfriend. By the way, from what I've seen, she's moved on to someone much better looking than you," I laughed hysterically.

See. I could be evil when I wanted to, I mentally patted myself on the back since my arms were currently occupied.

On my third round of moving boxes, Melkgard finally turned around, his distended, five arm body comically wrapped beneath a midnight blue apron. I narrowed my eyes in suspicion at the familiar fabric. He ignored my glare.

"Here you are, your last box of human parts. I hope they enjoy them," he gleefully chimed with a wicked smile.

I ignored his dripping maw and brought the last of the boxes outside the mountain where Zychor stood waiting. "Look at you. You've been working out, have you? Last I remember, you could barely hold onto the soul that got away," he roared in laughter.

My tail whipped in the direction of his face but he quickly ducked.

"You should visit more often, Dzik! Oh wait, you can't," he howled. "You can only visit once a week! Master's orders and all."

"Goodbye, Zychor," I mumbled under my breath before I reopened the portal and jumped through again and again with each crate, one at a time.

When the final crate was placed in the back room, I no longer heard the screams of torments or felt the flames of home. Any scraps of happiness I felt dissipated like the portal—into thin air. Time moved differently in the other realm. By the time I stacked the crates in the farthest corner of the room and re-emerged at the front of The Good Char, the only screams I heard were the cackles of teenagers and the only boils I saw were the pimples of these hormone-filled gangling humans.

Why, me? Why?

The master knew exactly what he was doing when he exiled me here for my punishment. I pulled up a folding chair to the counter, sat my flesh suit down and slammed my forehead on the counter with a sad groan, resigned to my fate.

"Hey, sir?" a squeaky voice floated from in front of me. "Are you open? I want a corndog."

CHAPTER 8

KIMMY

I FINALLY MADE IT HOME WHERE MY PARENTS WERE waiting for my arrival. Taking off my helmet and placing it on one of the side tables beside the front door, I looked at them curiously

"...Is everything okay?" I asked quietly, unsure if I should say anything at all.

Both of them had the look of disappointment etched across their faces and I gulped.

"Kimberly Anne, can you please come in here for a moment," my father commanded with an all familiar tone. When my parents came to this country to start a new life, they decided the best way to fully commit to assimilation was to give their daughter an Americanized name. I didn't like hearing it being said like this though.

My mother sat beside him, obediently, while

patting the chair beside them where a gift was sitting. It was wrapped in my favorite colors.

"That's for you," my father said with a huge smile. My heart raced as I made my way over. I couldn't wait to open it. I ripped through the decorated paper, revealing a brand new walkman. I squealed with utter joy before hugging my mother and father.

This was exactly what I wanted! All those late nights working at the restaurant, I was tired of being forced to listen to someone else's playlist. Now, I could listen to my own mixtape! I couldn't wait to use it at work.

Suddenly, my heart deflated a bit.

There had to be a catch. There was always a catch. As if in sync with my thoughts, my father opened his mouth to speak.

"Kimberly, you would never believe what I heard today."

I winced and braced myself.

"Is it true that you're dipping hotdogs for a job now? And just look at how you are dressed!"

His eyes bored into my tie-dye shirt and ketchup stain. My face flamed. I wasn't sure if I should cover myself or stand there obediently with my arms to my sides.

"You are single handedly trying to destroy the Ngo name which I fought so hard to build!" He hung his head in his hands dramatically and moaned.

"Harold, now, this is just a phase all teenagers

go through," my mother cooed, rubbing his leg. My parents decided later in life to change their names as well. "She's just trying to show some independence. She'll be back working at our restaurant soon."

"No," I blurted out, snapping both their heads in my direction. After my little taste of freedom, I couldn't go back to that. "I won't. I'm not coming back to the restaurant. I like where I work," I told them firmly, putting my metaphorical foot down. I wouldn't dare to do it physically. I liked living too much.

"Wait a minute. Who is your boss?" my dad asked with authority and I knew what was coming. "Is he a man? What does this man have over you? There has to be a reason why you are so dedicated to dipping hotdogs."

"I don't dip hotdogs, Dad. I dip weiners!" I raised my voice, blurting the first thing that came to my mind while I bolted up from my seat. Did it make any sense or difference? No, but that didn't matter. I needed to stand up for myself! *I swear, they aren't listening to anything I'm saying!*

"Oh my god. No, Harold, our little girl, she must be pregnant. It's the music she's been listening to, Harold," Mother said fervently. "Look at the pants and shorts she's wearing right now! Dipping weiners? That must mean sex. Kimberly Anne, you tell me right now, are you having sex? Harold, that's it," she cried. "She's pregnant!"

My father jumped up from his seat and began

pacing, threatening to wear a hole in the carpet. "Why me?" he called out to the ceiling. "Why would a daughter dishonor her father so terribly? She's pregnant by a hotdog dipper?"

I felt like I was going to die. What in the world was going on right now? How did we get here? "You sound just like Mr. Dzik. Chill out dad. I'm not having sex. I just like what I'm doing."

"Mr. Dzik?" His voice changed to a higher pitch and I grimaced. "My daughter works for someone named Dick! This is too much to bear. Why me, why me? Oh, the shame."

If parents had an oscar award for the most dramatic parent, he would win, hands down.

"If you aren't pregnant, what is it, baby? You can tell us anything," my mother pleaded. "Oh, no. That has to be it. She can't tell us because we will be accomplices." She covered her mouth dramatically and I rolled my eyes. "She killed someone!"

"What? No. I didn—"

"Harold, call our lawyer right now! We have to get her out of the country. Isn't your sister still visiting Sweden? Aren't they neutral? They can't expedite her if she's there."

"I didn't kill anyone!" I tried again to stop the nonsense. How did we end up here? "I just like my job. Are you even listening to yourselves?"

They both looked at me, puzzled, right before it started up again. "Now we know something is wrong. *No one* enjoys dipping weiners for a living!"

"That's it!" my father hollered then pulled out

his checkbook. "I'll pay him off for you. That has to be it. Margie, she must owe him money and she's working to pay off her debt." He paced around the room until he found a pen. "But you *will* pay me back every cent, young lady. Do you understand me?"

I swear my parents are mental. "I don't owe him any money! I haven't killed anyone and I'm not pregnant!—"

"It's drugs, isn't it?" my mom cut me off while standing there with her hands clasped in front of her, crying giant alligator tears. "Harold, look at her face. It's flush. That's one of the symptoms. My little girl is addicted to drugs. Is that why you turned down those scholarships to college? Baby, didn't you watch that commercial? Just say no."

"I cannot. I simply cannot!" I got up before they could drive me to insanity and walked to my room, slamming my door—as soft as I could— behind me.

My parents were delusional! But I valued living, not wanting to add to their ire. I could still hear them ranting in the living room. My mother was crying and my father was yelling 'why me'.

I needed to vent but I wasn't about to call Cindy, not with the way she treated me the other day! I groaned into my pillow. This was too much! This was exactly why I couldn't work with my parents anymore.

I laid across the bed angrily while I listened to them the rest of the night through the walls.

Drifting in and out of sleep, the sound of their voices turning into a hum in the back of my mind. Hugging my chibi plushie closer to my face, I positioned myself more comfortably when there was a knock at the door. Judging by the pattern, I knew exactly who it was. *My mother.*

Letting out a sigh, I listened to her sniffing on the other side. "Sweetheart, please talk to me. Tell me why are you doing this to us? Why are you going against us?"

"Against you?" I scoffed, incredulous. I pulled my face away from my pillow and stared at the closed bedroom door. "I'm just trying to live my life. Why would you think I'm going against you? I'm trying to love myself and find out who I am. I'm no longer that little girl, Mom. I'm grown up. It's time I spread my wings a little, don't you think?"

The door creaked open, revealing my mother with her hand still on the knob. We've always had a strange relationship. Sometimes she was overly caring, other times she wasn't caring enough. Too bad for me it was the former this time around.

"Sweetheart, just let me help you." How could she help me if she wasn't willing to listen to me? My mother, for all the good she tried to do in my life...still didn't know *me.*

Guilt hit me in the chest at the thought but it wasn't all my fault. I had rights too, didn't I? I was an adult for crying out loud.

"I don't need help. I just want you to accept me

for who I am. Why can't you just love me for who I'm trying to be, not the person you want me to be." I sat up on the edge of the bed, really looking at her. I couldn't believe how much I had been brainwashed under the guise of cultural expectations and obligations. I wasn't trying to be a bad daughter, I truly wasn't.

The only thing they wanted was for me to be what they wanted me to be. The realization hit me like an acme anvil falling from the sky. Communication would always be strained between us, our generations and environmental influences were worlds apart.

There was an awkward pause that only added to the tension already in the air. I was suffocating but I didn't want to kick her out of my room. I wasn't *that* kind of child.

She parted with a sad goodnight and I waited until she closed the door completely before removing the evidence from today. As irritating as my welcome home was... thinking over my first day at work, a smile still crept across my face.

Mr. Dzik was proud of me. He pointed out how impressed he was and I liked the feeling his praise gave me. My heart slowly hammered inside of my chest, threatening to claw its way out like the undead living inside of me. It was just my luck that Mr. Dzik was also nice to look at.

I shook my head and squealed against my pillow, forcing myself to sleep so that I could wake up bright and early for work tomorrow.

CHAPTER 9

THE SUN'S RAYS HIT MY FACE WITH A GENTLE WARMTH and I snapped my eyes open before blinking some of the sleep away.

It was time.

Biting my bottom lip, I rubbed my eyes and jumped out of bed, quickly going through my morning routine and peeking out my bedroom door.

The house was quiet. I strained my ears for a few more moments, making sure my parents had already left for the restaurant. Their hours of operations were much earlier than The Good Char and what once used to annoy me now worked to my advantage.

I wasn't sure if my mother would stay behind for another talk and as I tiptoed down the stairs, I was glad she didn't.

"Oh, I'm so excited. Another day as an independent woman!" I whispered to myself as I put on my helmet securely. Grabbing my bicycle, I walked it toward the sidewalk and hopped on, humming as I rode along the street, headed to my job and to see Mr. Dzik.

I had work to do and a job that I actually enjoyed. I spread my arms wide while pedaling, enjoying everything life had to offer. The sun was out and the air was fresh. It was a weekday and many of the neighborhood cars had already left their homes, leaving my neighborhood quiet.

The closer I got to the mall, the more the traffic picked up and I swerved as best I could away from them to make it to work safely. When I arrived at Hellscape Mall, the door was already unlocked for me by the friendly security guard. I gave him a bright smile and waved. His smile was a crooked one but it lit up his face as he welcomed me in.

I quickly made my way to the food court and watched as the other workers began to set up their bays. With a little skip to my step, I made it down to the very end, to my new little corner of joy.

"Hey, Mr. Dzik!" I called out, quickly grabbing my apron and putting it on with purpose.

"Hey. Get stuff prepped for service," he instructed gruffly without looking at me.

He put the wieners on the grill and I watched them rotate over and over, glazing until they got that good char. I couldn't help but notice that Mr. Dzik was wearing all black again under his apron. I wondered if he had any other colors in his closet.

Though, I shouldn't be wondering what was in his closet at all because now I was wondering what he looked like under his—

"There's a uniform for you in the corner. Put it on."

My eyes widened. *I'm official! This is it!* I jumped in place with my hands clasped in front of me, trying to contain my excitement.

I quickly excused myself to the back room and put on my uniform and hat. It fit me like a glove. How did he know my size so well? I came back out to the front and set up the cash register with more passion behind my movements.

I caught Mr. Dzik looking at me curiously and I sheepishly shrugged my shoulders. I couldn't help it.

My excitement was able to simmer as it was a slow morning, the weekday keeping a lot of patrons away until they got off work.

The silence between Mr. Dzik and I made me replay everything that happened with my parents last night in a loop. The longer I thought about it, the more frustration seeped into my being once again. I didn't like this feeling. I just wanted to be happy.

"Hey, Mr. Dzik—"

"It's Dzik."

"You'll never believe what my parents said about me working here."

"I don't care to know, just work," he said coldly.

He must be tired from opening up the store. I didn't blame him.

"They called you Mr. Dick, and they just couldn't understand that I enjoy working here with you. I appreciate having this job, truly. I look forward to coming in all the time, to, you know, work here, with you."

Embarrassment washed over me. I sounded like a dork. *Good job, Kimmy.*

He gave me a puzzled look, his jaw clenching and nostrils flaring. What I thought was a consti-pated look, I had come to find was something else. It must be his serious look. *I liked looking at his face.*

"Just work. I don't need to know," he gritted out again, completely ignoring what I was saying.

It reminded me of my parents. And now my frustration amped up a little more, my mouth rambling before I could control myself.

"They just want me to work at their restaurant and be under their thumb non-stop. I'm a woman and I don't need their approval to work where I want to work," I huffed, rolled my eyes and placed my hand on my hip. "I'm not a little girl anymore. No, sir. I am all woman. You know they asked me if I was on drugs and if I was pregnant? They had some nerve. I'm actually a really good person, Mr.Dzik."

His nostrils flared again and I blinked back my unshed tears. I didn't know why I was so emotional about all this. I shouldn't even be thinking about it. I should just enjoy working beside my nice boss and go about my day.

"Is your stuff ready for the lunch rush?" he said dryly. A quick glance at the clock told me we had about thirty minutes before it was time.

Why was he ignoring me? Maybe he was trying to keep things strictly professional and I could understand that. *I know he hears me and he cares about me. I can tell.*

Mr. Dzik went to the other side and began working the batter with the giant spoon. I watched as the muscles on his back and arms flexed. He was a very fit man. The more he worked the batter, the more I became lost in his rhythmic movements.

Look at him go! That was a man who was proud of his work. I admired that about him. Actually, I admired a lot about Mr. Dzik. My face flushed when I caught myself staring at his profile, hoping to catch a smile. I bet he had an amazing smile.

Get it together, Kimmy. You don't need to be looking at him like that, he's your boss.

Mr. Dzik's back tensed up right before he snapped his head over his shoulders to look directly at me. I blushed and giggle-coughed, before turning away, pretending to be busy dusting off the register.

An idea crossed my mind and I spontaneously went for it. I dropped my pencil onto the floor and slowly bent down to pick it up, to see if he would check me out the same way I did him. I mean, I think I had a nice, firm butt. Why wouldn't he look? When I finally picked it up and looked over my shoulder, he was already back to doing whatever he was doing on the other side.

Ugh. That was a major fail. Maybe I should just get back to work. *Serves you right, Kimmy.*

Embarrassment now laced my prior frustrations as I pulled up the stool, sat down, placed my chin in my hand and watched the patrons of Hellfire Mall make their way toward the food area with their arms full of shopping bags.

A couple of young boys came toward the counter.

"We should eat before we go meet the girls," I heard one of them say.

I straightened in my seat and offered them a kind smile, waiting for their order.

"Speaking of girls, how are you doing, pretty little thing. Do you have a boyfriend?" the second, older looking boy threw my way as he swaggered toward the counter and leaned in. He gave me a smirk that made his face look weird and I frowned in confusion when his demeanor immediately changed and he backed up.

Did I smell or something? I know I showered this morning and I didn't think I sweated too much on the ride here. I pretended to wipe my brow to discreetly smell myself. *No, I smell fine.*

"Either put in your order, or move out the way," came a deep, gruff voice over my head. I tilted my head back to see Mr. Dzik standing right behind me, focusing a laser glare directly at the two boys in front of me.

"Oh, Mr. Dzik! Did you want to take this order? Did you want to switch places?" I asked chirpily.

He had such a lovely, strong jaw from this angle—one that was currently flexing. I wonder what was bothering him? I straightened my head forward to see a new set of patrons in front of us. I guess the boys changed their minds, after all. Maybe they were late to their dates or something. Shrugging, I gave the next set of patrons a smile.

Mr. Dzik left and went to the back room grumbling. That was weird. I wondered what was up with him. Maybe he was having a bad day too. I didn't have time to ask him about it as the lunch rush started to line up at our counter.

"Mommy, Mommy! I want a corndog!" a cute little girl cried out, pulling her mother by the sleeve toward our counter.

I fulfilled a few of the orders alone since Mr. Dzik hadn't returned from the back. It was pretty easy. The fryer was vicious though. With my five feet three height, the oils threatened to slatter against the exposed skin on my neck. I quickly made my way back to the counter to take the next order: the little girl's.

"What are you doing?" Mr. Dzik barked behind me, making me jump in surprise.

I placed my hand on my chest and growled, turning to hit him on the arm. "Don't scare me like that! I almost felt my soul leave my body. Geez."

I quickly turned around with a smile and took the next order and ran to the fryer, placing the hot corndog on a paper tray and handing it to the customer.

"Thank you so very much. Come again!" I called out, waving at them. The little girl waved back with a face full of ketchup and cooked corndog batter. I giggled at the sight and my mood was lifted again.

Once the lunch rush began to die down, Mr. Dzik grabbed my arm and pulled me aside. I gave him a smile as I wiped my brow.

"That was a lot of hard work. We did it though! We make a great team, you and I."

"What were you doing near the grill?" he snapped irritably as if I kicked his imaginary dog, confusing me because he didn't look like the kind of guy to have a dog. "I told you to stay away from it!"

"I wasn't by the grill, really, I was by the fryer. I had to complete the orders. You were gone," I told him confidently.

He glared at me for a few seconds before shaking his head and releasing my arm. His hands were so large and warm. I kind of liked the way they felt on me. My face flushed again the moment the thought ran through my mind.

Mr. Dzik's eyes narrowed as I quickly made my way to obsessively clean the counter, hoping he didn't notice my reaction to him.

"Oh, it looks like I forgot a spot," I hummed.

Awkward silence.

I was sweating but I kept a smile on my face.

Oh, this was so embarrassing.

"Don't forget to clean around the fryer. You made a mess in your rush." His voice was softer this time around and I inwardly groaned.

He did notice.

"Yes, sir."

CHAPTER 10

DZIK

Dunking the piece in my hand into the vat of oil, I watched with satisfaction as the outer layer submitted to the boiling liquid. There was a strange gratification in watching flesh cook.

Memories of home and my time torturing souls appeased me during my punishment... until the sound of Kimmy Ngo sniffling and crying broke my concentration.

"I'm sorry!" Kimmy cried out with her bottom lip trembling like a freshly severed limb. My eye twitched. "I brought you what you asked for."

I glared beyond Kimmy's short stature to see another unsightly female pointing at my employee with an accusatory finger. She stood there with an air of audacity I despised beneath her sunglasses that overtook her revolting face. Her creature companion sat there, in her oversized bag, with his tongue lolling out the side, threatening to flick spittle onto my burnt, dipped offerings to the human realm.

I slammed the corndog that was in my grasp into the boiling vat, splashing the fiery oil onto my skin as I stomped in her direction. My skull tightened the longer I listened to her grating voice in front of my food bay. She was holding up the line as well as the other customers. I needed to get control of this situation quickly, seeing as my incompetent employee was doing nothing but sniveling at her metaphorical feet.

My claws itched to rip through my flesh suit so that I could pull her heart straight out of her chest cavity. But the master didn't need any more reason to add on to my sentence. What I decided to do instead was slam my hand on top of the counter while shoving Kimmy behind me.

"What seems to be the problem?" I snarled.

Her pathetic little creature in her bag whimpered and plopped his head into the darkness. The woman's eyes bulged right before she stuck her bulbous chest out and leaned toward me. Her ghastly forehead crinkled further as her face filled with disdain.

The feeling was mutual.

"Oh, so you're the hotdog dipper's boss. Figures. No wonder she messed up my order! What a waste of space."

"The only space being wasted right now is your distended gut, pressed against my counter," I growled as she gasped. "You either want what we offer here or you don't. Either way, you need to get out of my sight before I make more room in my fryer."

She sputtered and my back tensed when a soft touch came behind me. My nostrils flared at the over stimulation but I kept my eyes on the beast of a woman in front of me. It was imperative this despicable human knew who dominated this realm—The Good Char.

When Kimmy began petting my back, I could feel my tail want to burst forth in response.

"It was a mistake. I'm sorry," she whispered.

I gritted my teeth as I strained to listen to what the woman was saying.

The woman scoffed, before crossing her arms in front of her fleshy rolls while lowering her sunglasses to glare at me. "Mistake or not, I want another weiner, and I want it now."

I took a deep breath, imagining her skin peeling from her bones as her whole body caught on fire, before maintaining my composure. It was humans like this one that reminded me the master knew exactly what he was doing when he made my punishment in the realm of men.

I snatched the order slip from the counter and brought it to my face, reading it intently, wondering if I should grind her little furry companion into her meal. But as Kimmy's dainty little hands continued to stroke my back, I let out a frustrated sigh of discontent.

So the ingrate wanted a dipped weiner with mustard. I examined the weiner in question and noticed that the mustard was not the honey-based one we usually use.

How did Kimmy find this other mustard to begin with?

I stomped toward the back, grabbed a handful of honey-based mustard packets and slammed it in front of her. Leaning in, I made sure she felt every ounce of my fury through my pores. "Eat the flesh to your heart's content. Better yet, take your meat stick, like it and get out of my face!"

The woman glared at me. "How rude! I'll have you know—"

"Get the hell away from my shop before I make you!" I snarled and her beast cried out as if something was devouring it alive. One could only hope.

With a curl of my lip, I watched as the woman stormed out of our corner of the food court. If I ever saw that wretched piece of flesh again, I would make sure the demon of iniquity had more to play with back home.

I turned to find my employee sniffling and sniveling long after I ridded us of the issue. What was her problem? Why was water continuously leaking from her eyes if I had already expertly resolved things?

Kimmy wiped her face with the back of her hand and I scrunched my nose in disgust. Tilting my head upward, I counted the ugly sprites jumping in my mind to calm my nerves around this female. Sadly, I couldn't kill her. I still required her servitude to help make this sentence go by faster.

I sighed, realizing the earlier incident would affect her deeply. Of course, it would. The master probably planted her here for that purpose to drive me to insanity.

She nodded as if I said something and responded with a shaky voice that made my insides feel like they were being shredded with a serrated blade from the underworld. "I'm fine, Mr. Dzik. Just a bit shaken up."

"Just get the mopping done and make sure it's clean," I told her.

Kimmy smiled as she always did, even through her tears. What was it about this female that made her operate out of the realms of what humans normally did?

"Thank you, boss. I'll make sure to double-check every order from now on," she promised softly.

I patted her shoulder awkwardly with two fingers, trying to keep her at a distance. "Mistakes happen. Unluckily, no one was killed. I appreciate your hard work. Now, clean up this mess and disinfect the floor."

Kimmy nodded again before obediently grabbing a mop. Her willing servitude toward me was invaluable. I needed to be more careful. Chaining her to the backroom until the next work day wouldn't work well in the long run. These blasted humans, like the wretched woman that was here, were known to pick up the nearest payphone and call the local authorities.

Going back to frying the rest of the corndogs, I imagined the fun I would have with little Kimmy if we were back home. To rip her body in half and plunge her flesh into the magma available through the mountains would be quite a sight.

I wonder if she would enjoy my company then? Would she continue to harbor her smiles toward me? She shouldn't look as pleasing as she did through her tears, because now I wondered if her screams of agony would actually sound more like screams of gratitude if I—

"Mr. Dzik? I mopped the floor, anything else I can do?"

Quickly pulled from my strange daydream, I turned to look at her wet face. Kimmy was still sobbing while sweeping. I scowled. Now I would have germs all over my floor. I needed to disinfect them again just to make sure...

Grabbing the broom from her hands, I pointed at the stool and silently commanded her to stay in one place while I cleaned the rest of this place again. As I snapped on my black, elbow length gloves and grabbed a bottle of bleach I realized I had never seen her this frazzled before. I didn't think she was even capable of being anything but disgusting sunshine.

I wondered what else was going on with her...

CHAPTER II

KIMMY

Walking my bicycle to the side of the house, I could feel my shoulders droop from the day's events. I leaned my mode of transportation against the wall before slowly making my way to the front door, my mind still whirring over what the woman said to me, my mistake, and how I clammed up in response.

If it wasn't for Mr. Dzik, I would have melted to the floor like the wicked witch from all her glaring and harsh words. But he saved me. He saved my dignity as he expertly took over and handled everything with ease.

I mean, I wouldn't have personally chosen some of his words but the results were the same.

Exhaustion consumed my every step as I trudged up the few porch stairs toward the sanctuary of my house. My body ached from all the cleaning I had to do after the ordeal, and my mind yearned for a moment of respite. I was glad to be away from the crowd for once, though there was a slight longing for Mr. Dzik's constant presence to give me a sense of security. I couldn't very well bring him home with me though and I couldn't stay there after the store was closed.

With a deep exhale, I turned the doorknob and crossed the threshold without looking. Little did I know, I was entering into a lion's den of parental interrogation. They wasted no time in bombarding me with their incessant and pessimistic questions.

"So, have you managed to embarrass our family today?"

The words pierced me like a dagger to my chest. My day was already rough, and now I had to come home to this? Was it truly this hard to be an independent woman? How did everyone do it?

Maybe that was why most of the other Asians I knew in the neighborhood continued to help with their family business even beyond marriage.

I tried my best to ignore the way her words made me feel. Did she purposely choose those words to be her first? More than likely. But I had to keep in mind that they never once gave me their approval and that it was me who went behind their back to make this decision.

Without talking back, I made my way toward my room quietly with my head hung down.

"I've had enough," my father said with a

chilling finality. "Young lady, turn around and stand before me this instant."

My back tensed and my hand froze on the railing. My heart pounded inside of my chest and my mouth went dry. Blinking back a few unshed tears, I took a deep breath and did as I was told.

Fear coiled inside of my gut like a snake ready to strike and take me down. I wanted to be brave. I wanted to stand up for my choices. I couldn't go back to the restaurant, not after the way Mr. Dzik stood up for me. He deserved a stronger employee and I was willing to work hard to become that.

I reluctantly approached my father and made extra sure to not drag my feet loudly. I took a discreet deep breath inward and exhaled through my mouth while keeping my eyes casted downward.

"I will no longer stand idly by while you tarnish my name. Either you quit that job of hotdog dipping or you are disowned," he spat, jabbing a finger in my face. I could only imagine his scowl etched across his face. Their disapproval made it hard for me to breathe through my nose.

My heart stopped.

"Harold, please don't say that," my mother pleaded with a broken voice.

I watched as my tears dripped onto the floor and part of my shoe. Biting my bottom lip, I swallowed all my words down and tried to force myself to think of the day, I would finally fly from this nest that was threatening to suffocate me.

I knew my parents loved me. How could they not. But it was moments like this, I didn't think I could survive much longer. It was why I always chose to see the brighter side of things. Because life was just a sequence of choices, wasn't it? I wanted so desperately to choose a happier way.

I could feel his fiery gaze burn into the top of my head. "Kimmy. What is your choice?"

I closed my eyes and let the rest of the tears fall as the words slipped from my lips, barely audible. "I'm moving out."

I then did something my younger self would never have been brave enough to do. I sniffed, turned away, and retreated toward my room without waiting to be dismissed.

Their voices blended into a cacophony of argument as I ascended the hallway.

"Harold! What have you done? With her background of possible murder and drug use, you're going to throw her onto the streets? Oh no, our baby will be forced to strip for dollars, Harold! What are you doing to my only daughter?" my mother wailed in despair.

"She made her decision. Now she will live with it. You have forty-eight hours, and I expect a well written two week notice to be handed to me for my approval," my father called out after me, his voice echoing through the house right before I quietly shut my bedroom.

Placing my head against the door, I sniffed and

hugged myself as I continued to eavesdrop on their muffled argument below.

"Oh, Harold. Our baby can't survive on the unforgiving streets. She'll simply wither away and die. What would happen to our lineage? Don't you want grandchildren to pass our family name? How could you?" she cried.

"You worry too much, Margie," he chastised her. "You know that girl knows she won't make it out there without us. You might as well make room in the back offices again for her return. Our restaurant has missed her meticulous way of bookkeeping. She'll see, soon enough, that all of this is just a phase. We'll be alright."

A phase? How could he call my need for independence a phase? I couldn't be the only twenty three year old in this world with the same desires.

I gritted my teeth and softly planted my fist against the door beside my face. What would Mr. Dzik do? He was so brave, so courageous, so strong. I needed to pull from his strength today.

Panic coursed through my veins at the thought of really going through leaving. I never wanted it to be this way. I always dreamt of my move day as a happy experience with my mother gushing over what kind of furniture we needed to buy in order to match the table I was probably going to pick up from a rummage sale one of these days.

But as much as I tried to convince myself of positive outcomes, I knew in the back of my mind this was a possibility. That was why I had already researched what I needed to do in order to move into my first apartment.

With a dry gulp, I pulled my head away from the door, wiped my face and pulled up my big girl panties. How much money did I have in my savings? In a frenzy, I dashed toward my kitty bank and hopped onto the edge of my bed. Turning it over to its cute little belly, I pulled out the rubber stopper and reached in with my little fingers, digging around and patiently pulling out all its contents.

Frantically, I rummaged through the scattered coins, and neatly rolled and bound up wads of cash. I counted them with trembling hands, my eyes burning with tears at what had to be done.

I sniffed and flicked my gaze to the door, listening intently. I didn't hear any more arguments, so I quietly counted the grand total of what I had.

"Nine-hundred dollars," I whispered. What were the odds? The perfect amount without any trailing cents. It was meant to be. It had to be now. Now or never.

I had always been the one to turn to when my classmates needed to cheat on their math test and now the skill was to my advantage. According to my calculation, I needed the amount for the first month, a deposit, and possibly a deposit for light and water. Yes, no one ever died without water. I needed water. That was enough to get me through to the next paycheck. *Thank you Mr. Dzik for taking a chance on me.*

I knew there was a reason why you came into my life. If only Cindy could see me now. She wouldn't dare make fun of me anymore. I was going to be Mrs. Independent!

Missus.

Who would I be a missus to?

Flashes of Mr. Dzik in his black outfit and his corndog apron came before me and I could feel my face flame.

"Calm down, Kimmy. One thing at a time. You can't put the horse in front of the carriage."

I sniffed. I didn't even have a carriage. My trusty bicycle would have to do, for now.

Looking over my treasure once again, I felt my courage swell within my chest. "That should be more than enough to find a place," I beamed, a spark of determination igniting within me.

I would show them both that I was capable of standing on my own two, size six and a half, feet.

CHAPTER 12

THE NEXT MORNING, I ARRIVED AT WORK BRIGHT AND early, eager to establish my newfound independence. I wasted no time in diving into my tasks, starting with washing all the walls and scrubbing away every smudge and stain. After that, I meticulously cleaned out the bucket and disinfected the counters, ensuring every surface was spotless. With a sense of liberation in my heart, I began to whistle the tune of "Walking on Sunshine."

No longer under the oppressive rule of my parents, I was a free woman, determined to prove myself and secure my place in the world.

As I hummed my tune, Mr. Dzik snapped his head to mine while holding onto a still sizzling corndog that came straight out the fryer. I was getting used to his resting glower face, so I thought nothing of it and continued cleaning happily.

"What's wrong with you? Why are you here so early, and why are you so happy?"

Oh, he was so nosy, it was cute. I think he had a communication problem. His growly words translated in my mind that he was curious about my change in demeanor. I mean, I would be too.

Grinning from ear to ear, I tried to contain my excitement but failed miserably... or happily, depending on how one looked at it. "Well, Mr. Dzik, we get paid on Fridays, right? I mean, I've only gotten a couple of paychecks so far and that seems to be the trend. It's new to me since my parents always gave me allowances growing up and with me helping with the accounting at work, it slips my mind if I get paid alongside the employees at the same time or not. Anyway! I need this job because last night I totally stood up to my parents, and now I'm looking for apartments!"

I squealed and did a little dance with the broomstick, twirling around it with flare.

My little jig was interrupted with the sound of a large quantity of corndogs being thrown into the fryer, sizzling and spitting oil everywhere. It didn't stop the emotion bubbling up as I smiled at Mr. Dzik's back, watching the way his muscles moved when he shook the frying cage with ease.

"You talk too much."

He's such a jokester.

Undeterred by his lack of enthusiasm, I carried on with my duties, cleaning and disinfecting every inch of the business. The scent of pine cleaner filled the air as I mopped the floor, sweat trickling down my forehead.

As the day progressed, a line of customers formed. Wiping my brow, I made sure to keep my composure as I took orders and relayed them to my corndog partner in crime.

"One weiner with ketchup and mustard," I yelled, and like a well-oiled machine, Mr. Dzik swiftly prepared the order.

Hours passed, and we continued this dance of weiner creation and customer satisfaction. Side by side, Mr. Dzik and I formed the perfect team, delivering delicious breaded weiners to the hungry patrons of Death Canyon City.

"Phew, this is quite a workout," I commented, wiping the sweat from my brow and the back of my neck, but this time with a clean towel.

Without a second thought, I impulsively pulled off my shirt, revealing the black tank top I always wore underneath. Mr. Dzik's face contorted into a combination of his resting glower face, constipation and something else I couldn't identify.

I hoped he was okay. Maybe he ate something bad.

"Put your uniform back on!" he barked, before shaking his head and curling his lip.

Realizing my mistake, I squeaked and quickly complied. Except when I slipped my shirt back on, it was a little bit difficult to maneuver when the wet parts slapped onto my skin. Eww. But despite his rebuke, I couldn't help but feel a glimmer of satisfaction. Mr. Dzik had noticed my hard work and dedication. I utilized every yoga move I knew to try and make redressing comfortable, wriggling my way awkwardly like a bad circus act all the way toward the register.

When my body finally warmed up the shirt, I was able to relax while I occasionally pulled away the fabric to fan myself. Who knew selling corn-dogs would be such a workout? At least my summer body wasn't as far away as I thought.

I laughed out loud at my thoughts, making my boss' head snap in my direction again. I sheepishly ducked my head, telling myself it was ridiculous to think about a summer body when The Flaming Chopstick in the same food court was my weakness.

I wonder if Mr. Dzik would consider that betrayal for grabbing food from there. I discreetly looked in his direction but his back was already to me again. As much as I loved his dipped wieners, smelling it day in and day out, I couldn't stomach eating it all the time. Not that Mr. Dzik was bad at handling wieners. He was great at dipping the meat.

I mean.

Oh gosh.

Stop while you're ahead, Kimmy.

Too late. My eyes zoomed in on the bulging veins of his forearms as he stabbed some of the corndogs into the frying oil.

Whew, was it hot in here again?

"You've worked hard today."

"Wh-What?" I stammered, quickly averting my

eyes to catch his glaring at me. I wasn't sure if I should take his words as praise or a negative statement of fact. Working hard was a good thing, right? It was what my parents always hammered into my head.

I opened my mouth to spit out an involuntary apology, when he cut me off.

"Good job."

My eyes fluttered a few times as my face flamed at his praise. I mean, getting praise at all was new to me. I didn't get much from my parents and now I feel spoiled by Mr. Dzik. He needed to be careful. If he did it too much, I might get addicted to it.

"You know..." he drew out as he turned his back to me again, returning to check on the weiner's rotation on the grill.

My heart pounded at the pregnant pause. No, I didn't know. What was he going to say? Was he going to praise me again? Oh gosh. I began to perspire at the back of my neck. My shirt felt too tight, too wet. But I couldn't take it off to cool down. I didn't want him mad at me. I wanted him to enjoy working with me. I hope I didn't do anything wr—

"You can go home early, full pay."

A squeal left my lips before I could stop myself. I jumped and clapped with delight, almost throwing myself into his arms—almost.

I didn't want him to feel how sweaty I was. Yes. That was right. That was why I didn't go through with it. But my gosh, what an amazing man he was! So kind. Despite his growly exterior that always looked like he wanted to strangle everyone who spoke to him, he did care about me! And he appreciated all my efforts.

Mrs. Independent was here to stay!

"Thank you, Mr. Dzik!" I exclaimed, my voice filled with genuine gratitude. "I promise every day I will be an asset to your business and your company."

Giggling like a schoolgirl, I nimbly folded my apron, placed it on the back counter and made my way out into the food court. The breeze hitting my neck wasn't enough. I was too excited and it amped up my internal temperature. Finally taking off my shirt again, I tucked it into the back pocket of my pants and retied my pony tail into a bun to get the wayward strands off my neck.

Fanning myself, I walked with a pep to my step as I made it out of the mall and hopped on my bike. I pedaled my way home with the wind in my hair —I felt as free as a bird.

All thanks to the kindness of Mr. Dzik.

"I was free as a bird now and something something," I sang, unsure of the words to the song but continued to sing it anyway with enthusiasm. "You paid with a five so here's your change.... you paid with a five so here's your changeeeeeee."

I laughed aloud at my made up lyrics as I continued to ride through the streets. The world was my oyster, and with each pedal, I embraced the possibilities that lay ahead. No longer bound by the constraints of my parents' expectations, I was determined to carve out my own path, one filled with adventure at the side of Mr. Dzik.

Who knew what the future held, but one thing was certain—I was ready to take on the world with a smile on my face and a song in my heart.

CHAPTER 13

DZIK

The sun was shining outside as usual in this wretched city. I could still feel Kimmy's bright aura as she left the bay. My skin always prickled in awareness when she was around. It pissed me off. I had enough of her happiness for the day so I decided to make her leave for my own sanity.

I tied my apron again and prepared myself for the bustle of the evening rush. There was about an hour left before we closed and last minute hungry customers would soon be flocking to my stand. Like roaches, the rush began, weaving around Kimmy as she once again removed her coverings. Office workers and tourists alike flocked to me, all eagerly placing their orders for dipped weiners made of human flesh.

The sizzle of the fryer was a constant background buzz as hungry eyes and growling stomachs stood at the ready. The aroma of cooked flesh wafted through the food court and I wickedly grinned as Justin glared at me from his bay.

Disappointingly, the sound of something I hated more than Kimmy's singing floated toward me—a group of rowdy teenage boys.

They were a motley crew of boiled-faced kids, their laughter echoing through the food court. Triumphing over Justin's disgusting pastry treats out of my mind, I glowered in the direction of these gangling humans as they approached my counter.

Dealing with ingrates like these made for longer days during my sentence. My fingers itched to rip their flesh and devour it as I jammed their bones into their orifices, cackling with mirth as I listened to their screams of agony.

Once the boils were peeled off, their flesh would be the same as the others once grounded together. I debated whether I should donate a few bodies to Melkgard. The master wouldn't notice a few extra souls, surely.

"Whoooo! You see that chick that walked by with the black hair? I can show her a thing or two," one of them laughed.

Vile creatures. The master knew exactly what he was doing when he placed me in this teenage trap to be tortured by the idiots of the flock. I would rather deal with the ancient ones walking in circles than—

"Yeah, I promise you all I need is three minutes and a rubber," The other one replied before slapping their hands together in the air in a strange human custom referred to as a high five.

Why they were celebrating something that apparently hadn't happened was beyond me.

Idiots, the lot of them.

"I bet we could catch up to her. I've seen her here before. She's got a bicycle parked out in front. Let's grab some corndogs and go after her. Heck, maybe she'll take some more clothes off," the third one crowed after wagging his eyebrows.

My nostrils flared as I shoved the latest order into the guy's chest, pushed him aside and shot out my arm to grab the scruff of the closest idiot's shirt.

"Who exactly are you looking at?" I growled, reading to take a bite out of the tip of his nose and spit it back in his face.

"I-I—" the idiot stammered and I threw him against the other one, knocking them both down.

Calmly, I stepped from behind the counter and made my way toward the third who was backing away slowly with his hands raised in supplication. I could feel my flesh suit threaten to tear the more I closed the distance.

I watched with scrutiny as his Adam's apple bobbed from a dry swallow before he stood his ground and pretended to face me without fear. His wavering voice said otherwise. "H-Hey, man, give me a weiner with extra pickles and cheese."

The rest of the patrons who stood behind them began to back away and disperse. Good riddance. I would feed them their own flesh another day. They would be back. They always came back like lambs to the slaughter.

I stared at this pimple-faced meat sack before pointing at the menu which clearly stated the options available.

"We don't have pickles or cheese as toppings," I gritted out slowly, enunciating each word.

The teenager frowned and turned to his friends with false bravado. "Did you hear that, guys? This guy doesn't have pickles or cheese! What kind of weiner place is this?"

The other two, now back on their feet, let out humorless laughs.

"Come on man, let's just go and grab something from The Flaming Chopstick," one of them whispered, keeping his eyes averted.

Pathetic.

Once they all scrambled away, I returned behind the counter and crossed my arms, glaring in their direction.

Time clicked by slowly and I debated whether to follow them after they left the mall. I would show them exactly what I could do with a piece of rubber... and the flames of hellfire.

"I want a weiner with avocado and bacon on top."

Snapping my eyes to the customer in front of me, I curled my lip without offering a response. Flexing my forearms to hold myself back from murder, my muscles rippled beneath my flesh suit, the skin on my back beginning to tear beneath my clothes.

I wouldn't hear the end of it if the other guys heard about random corndog murder scenes that led to my temporary prison being shut down. I could only imagine what other punishments the master would have in store for me. The Good Char was already sending me over the edge. I'd sooner jump into a vat of fire before being placed some-where like that foul store on the other side of Hellscape Mall that looked as though a pink monster exploded and painted the interior with its entrails.

The teenager scoffed, refusing to leave my presence. "Come on, man! Don't you know anything about gourmet hotdogs? Avocado and bacon are the way to go!"

My eye twitched right before my hand shot out with a crunch right into his face. His body flopped like the dead as he landed face first into the floor, eliciting gasps of horror around us.

"Someone call an ambulance!"

"What are they fighting over?"

"Weiners..."

I leaned over the counter and snarled at his unconscious form. "You should thank me. You won't be able to see your boils anymore, just a fist print. Anything else with that knuckle sandwich?" I grinned.

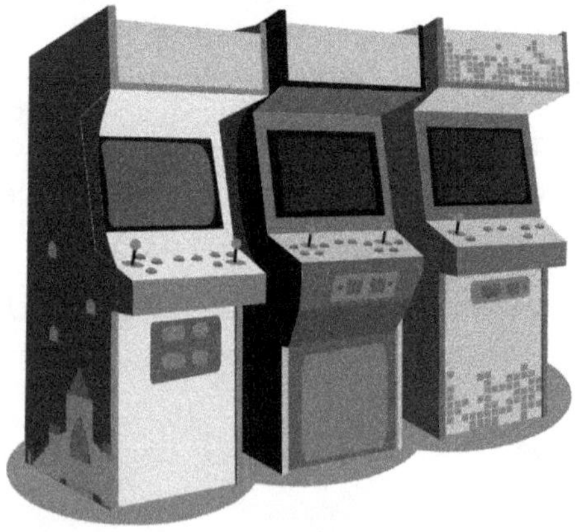

CHAPTER 14

KIMMY

My new apartment was sparse, but it was the best I could do while divvying up the money I currently had appropriately. I needed to play it smart if I was to be successful.

If my parents found out I snuck out to buy an apartment and failed, I wouldn't be able to live it down. It would be worse than when they found out about me working at The Good Char.

"What now, Kimmy? You got a roof over your head and a chair that came with the apartment. How are you going to sleep?" A few tenants scurried across the room's floor. Ewww, okay, bug spray was a must. When one ran up the wall, I watched him like a hawk and screamed as it took flight.

I bit my bottom lip and sucked in my pride. There was no way around it. I was going to have to stay at my parents house. These flying creatures gave me the heebie jeebies. That settled it, I needed a few more days to figure something out. Maybe I could look up used furniture in the paper, just for the time being.

I cringed at the thought of a used mattress. Who knew what kind of cooties it had?

"Ugh!"

I threw my hand in the air before hanging my head. Maybe I was going to have to stay with my parents for another month, save up some more money while working for Mr. Dzik.

I wanted to cry. My dreams deflated as I slowly backed away and locked the door to my apartment. Sniffing, I wiped my eyes with my sleeve and startled when I saw a man down the hall stare at me. He gave me a soft smile and I gave one back before leaving the building in embarrassment at having been caught in my feelings in front of a stranger.

I needed to make sure I saved face despite how much of a mess I was feeling on the inside. I didn't need anymore gossip to reach my parents' ears.

Swinging my leg over my bicycle seat, I pedaled back to my parents' house and let the air dry the tears on my cheeks.

Walking my bicycle to the side of the house, I internally gave myself a pep talk before I walked through the front door.

My parents sat at the kitchen table, my mother sipping her tea quietly as my dad flipped through the newspaper. No words were exchanged as I nimbly walked up the stairs with as little sound as possible and prepared for a shower.

I needed to relax my muscles and wash away the evidence of the day. In fact, I lost my appetite on the way here with thoughts of how much cooking tools would cost for my new apartment.

Maybe Mr. Dzik will allow me to take some of the leftover corndogs home after the shop closes. I never knew what he did with them and assumed he just threw them away because he always made a new batch when I arrived.

Massaging my scalp, I yelped in surprise when my restroom door slammed open.

"Kimmy, don't you think this has gone on long enough?" came my mother's voice.

With my hands placed over my soapy private parts, I stared through the privacy glass door of my shower.

"W-What do you mean? Mom, I'm showering right now. Can't this wait?" I pleaded. But to my dismay, she lowered the toilet lid and sat down. What was happening right now?

"You, working for a man! You have been acting so strange. I think I know what it is, your maternal instincts are kicking in. Of course, they are, with the age you are. You're waiting too long. And if this is a need you are trying to fulfill, just let me know. Mrs. Chen, our favorite customer, has been telling us about her handsome and wealthy son who had gone back to the motherland to help out his aunt. He is a good boy, the kind of boy that would be good for you. He's a lawyer too. He knows about sacrifice. You can't keep working with someone we haven't heard much about at the mall. It's unsightly, Kimmy. Think of the family."

She gasped dramatically and I braced myself for the next frantic onslaught.

"Have you been doing sex things with your boss?" she wailed.

"Mom!"

"Kimmy! Men are predatory creatures who only want to do things with you for a few minutes and then you are stuck with them. They'll take you and while you are staring up at the ceiling the next thing you know they're snoring and you have to pretend it was amazing."

Were we still talking about me? Good grief! I needed to stop her before I begged the universe to swallow me whole. "Are we really doing this? Please! Have mercy. I need to shower!"

"What will your father say? He will blame me for raising you this way because you are a daughter and I am your mother. Would you do that to me? I can't be the talk of the town. We've worked too hard to build what we have. How can you not think of us, Kimmy?"

I stopped responding. It was no use. I was still full of soap and the water was beginning to cool.

She continued a few more minutes about disgrace and her struggle with saving face when some of the other families were asking her about when I was going to get married and bring forth children.

"All I could think about were hotdogs. You can't make children with hotdogs, Kimmy! You need stability like what the restaurant offers. Or through marrying a doctor or a lawyer like Mrs. Chen's son. You need to keep on track so your eggs don't dry up by the time you find a man. Kimmy! Are you listening to me?"

I sighed and continued to shower despite having an audience. There was no way around it. "Yes, Mom."

She rambled as I finished up washing my hair in silence besides a few mumbles of 'yes'. Finally, tired of berating me through a shower door, she huffed then got up and left.

My heart was on the floor, swirling in the drain with the rest of the water as I turned it off and stepped out to grab a towel.

I chuckled to myself as I thought about how sweaty I was today, desperately wanting to cool to finally coming home... to a cold shower because my mother refused to let me shower in peace.

"Just a month, Kimmy. Maybe a few weeks. You can do this," I whispered to myself as I wiped my hand across the foggy glass cabinet.

Red rimmed my eyes and I sniffed, wiping them with the towel before taking a deep breath and truly staring at my reflection, wondering when it would show who I truly was on the inside—who I truly believed I could be, Mrs. Independent.

Quietly, I got dressed in my pajamas as my mother called my name from the first floor, letting me know there was food ready.

I couldn't stomach it. Not after her lecture. And I couldn't face my dad who possibly had his own lecture waiting.

I towel dried my hair as best as I could before sitting at the edge of my bed, staring out my window into the darkness.

Was my mother right? Was it more imperative of me to think of a future, a husband and bringing forth a family? I couldn't swallow the fact that I would be bringing them into this vicious cycle of always struggling to survive through family business. What if my child had different aspirations and dreams? What if my child was like me?

How could I tell her she was in the land of the free where dreams came true if I didn't lead by example in pursuing my own?

I let my body fall back and turned to my side.

My mother called for me again but I closed my eyes, letting a tear fall onto the sheet.

"I'm sorry," I whispered.

CHAPTER 15

DZIK

Despite her constant smiles, something was lacking. I should be celebrating the fact that her obnoxious sunshine attitude was toned down but a new disturbance curled in my gut, one that wouldn't leave me alone.

"Kimmy, man the fryer. I need to grab something from the back," I commanded.

Her soft brown eyes widened into saucers as she startled and then gave me a weird little salute.

Grumbling to myself about strange human behavior, I rummaged through some of the supplies when I heard a screech. My feet led me out before my mind could decide whether I truly cared.

Back home, I was known to be one of the least remorseful demons around. So I was flummoxed when I found myself grabbing my little employee and carrying her to the sink where I promptly shot her arm full of high pressure cold water. The spray of liquid hit us both in various ways but my body moved instinctively as I quickly grabbed a towel and wrapped her forearm which was reddening as the seconds ticked by.

"What in the blazes have you done?" I barked out louder than I probably should.

Her whimper tore at something inside of me and I turned off the neon sign and pulled her into the back room, sitting her on stacks of flour as I begrudgingly rummaged through the human first aid supplies.

"I'm so sorry, Mr. Dzik. I don't know what happened. I mean, it happened so fast, I can't remember how I slipp—"

"For the love of hellfires, stop prattling and sit still!" I growled as I stomped my way toward her, slamming the first aid kit beside her hip and pulled out whatever this antibiotic ointment was and then wrapped her arm until I ran out of the material. I had the need to kill someone but kept my hands occupied as I grabbed some of the premade ice, placed it in a towel and stomped back beside her, placing the wretched thing on top of her injury.

Movement caught my eye and I snapped my head up to see her bottom lip trembling. Her comically large eyes were shining, telling me she wanted to talk but couldn't because I commanded her not to.

Was it wrong of me to feel a bit of satisfaction at that fact? I very much liked her not jabbering my ear off.

But when a wayward tear escaped her left eye, I scowled. Why was she still crying? Haven't I already fixed the problem? My eyes shot to her arm and then back to her face, then back to her arm. What in the blazes was wrong with this human? Has she malfunctioned because of a fryer burn? How in the world did she manage to splash herself when the curated flesh was contained with a metal basket before one even dipped it into its vat of torture?

Her lip trembled once more as the bottom of her eyes began to rim red. Then she hung her head in silence. My chest constricted uncomfortably as if I was having the worst case of heartburn after devouring a foul sprite.

"What?" I roared. "What is it?!"

She shook her head and I was about to explode out of my flesh suit from sheer frustration. Why wasn't she saying anything? How hard was it to answer the damn question?!

"I-I should have been more careful when I dropped th-the basket. Please, don't be mad at me, Mr. Dzik. I can still work the rest of the shift, I swe—"

I slapped my hand over her mouth and curled my lip. "If you can't manage the fryer, all you had to do was say so!"

Her eyes shone again against the light but the

atmosphere shifted. A new scent invaded the air, cloaking the room with a mixture of fear and... feminine musk.

My nostrils flared as I continued to stare at her, wondering what kind of witchcraft she was spinning this time. The more I inhaled her scent, the more my true skin prickled into spikes, wanting to burst free from its confines in more ways than one.

I could mentally feel my tail swishing back and forth, grateful I couldn't hear it physically knocking over supplies in this room.

I slowly sat down beside her, staring in suspicion as I inched my hand away from her mouth a bit at a time. Before I could fully remove my fingers, I leaned in and took a deep whiff behind her ear. Her sharp inhale made the hairs on the back of my neck stand on end, anticipating an attack—or the master jumping out and cutting my head off with his scythe for entertainment.

When Kimmy bit her bottom lip, I growled but didn't get another word in when she bolted to her feet and ran out the room, leaving me sitting there dumbfounded. It was as if she vacuumed the scent out with her and it made me irrationally angry.

Getting to my feet, I quietly put the first aid supplies away and exited the room, watching her every movement as she busied herself with the customers, waving her injured arm like a war trophy.

Snarling at her pointed ignoring of me, I grabbed a handful of human flesh on a stick, dunked them into the batter and threw them into the fryer to watch them burn. Glaring at the ignorance of the humans around us, I mentally willed her to look at me.

Her back tensed but she quickly straightened and took the next order, avoiding my gaze as she fulfilled it on her own like a little fairy—repulsive little things akin to sprites—floating around the shop.

Ten customers in and I could feel steam coming off my skin. And no, it wasn't from the oil burns I sustained keeping my eyes on Kimmy's back, waiting for her to acknowledge me.

During the next temporary lull, she deftly maneuvered her dark mane in strange patterns until it was tied up in a messy pile on top of her head. The only problem was, the moment she fanned herself with one of our menus, that same feminine musk hit my nose and embedded itself into my pores, refusing to let me go.

"Enough!" I growled, stomping beside her and slamming the 'Sorry, we're closed' sign on the counter before turning off the neon lights once again. I lowered my face to hers, took a long inhale and gritted out, "meet me in the back in the next two minutes."

She gulped and nodded her head before scrambling to take off her little apron. Refusing to give her the satisfaction of knowing that I was practically preening at her attention, I breathed through my mouth as I waited for her in the back with my arms crossed, ready to verbally tear her limb from limb.

The only problem was, when she entered, she also took off her outer top layer, showcasing her glistening globes under my scrutiny.

Running a frustrated hand down my face, I debated whether I should just throw her into the grill's vortex to be rid of her or run my tongue down the valleys that taunted me, shining with perspiration from the work day.

"What the blasted hell is wrong with you today? Why are you acting differently? Is there something I need to know? Something you need to —" I narrowed my eyes once again in suspicion, still unconvinced the master didn't plant her here for my destruction. "—tell me."

"I-I don't know what you mean. I'm just working as hard as I always do, Mr. Dzik. I promise. If I'm failing at something, just let me know and I'll rectify it. Did you see how happy our customers were? We're such a great team. I bet we'll sell out all of our prepared supplies today, don't you think? All in a good day's work, right?"

She laughed awkwardly and averted her gaze to something behind me. I turned and saw nothing that would interest her, leaving me baffled as to what exactly was transpiring.

I leaned in, trying to stare into her soul to see if I could force the truth out of her. "I don't like what's going on, Kimmy. I'm going to ask you to leave work early today and return when you get your head back on straight," I threatened.

Only, she didn't see it the same way.

"Really?" she gasped, clasping her hands in front of her with a hidden smile I couldn't decipher. "You are always so kind to me, Mr. Dzik. I am feeling a bit frazzled today because I just got this new place and there's been some complications. I'm just trying to get control of everything that's happened in my life and I guess I'm not in control as I thought I was. I mean, I don't know exactly how to explain it but I can't give up, you know? And every time you're kind to me like this, my heart just wants to explode. You don't know how much it means to me to be able to have a few moments to slip away and... sort things out. Even if it's just in my mind. I don't know how I'll ever repay you but I promise I will. Thank you. Thank you for being there for me."

My mind was still trying to catch up with her rapid fire words when she caught me by surprise, pressing her soft lips to the flesh of my cheek. I froze, confused, befuddled, angry, irritated, then furious as I straightened... only to catch a glimpse of her mess of a mane and her back as she left me standing there alone once again unsure of what just transpired.

CHAPTER 16

KIMMY

THE NEXT DAY STARTED THE SAME. MY BOSS HAD already set everything up upon opening before I got there. All I had to do was sit behind the register obediently, waiting for customers to line up. We didn't say much to each other this time around. I was embarrassed at my behavior yesterday and couldn't find the courage to start a conversation.

You practically told him your whole life already. It was a good thing the burn wasn't bad, even though he treated you like your flesh was peeling. It was beyond adorable.

I giggled to myself and schooled my features when he walked by, avoiding looking at him.

It was the weekend and the early mornings brought in more patrons today. People began to gather in the food court sporadically, the voices of children whining and some babies crying floated through the air. It was going to be a long day, I could already tell.

Usually, I was excited to start the day but something was off. Perhaps it was the residual feelings from my parents who still gave me disappointed looks when they were home and the strange reaction I had to Mr. Dzik that threw me off today.

I leaned over the counter and gave everyone around us a welcoming smile the way I always did. A few of the shoppers caught sight of me, smiled back and made their way over. The first order was four corndogs and two pink lemonades.

I yelled over to Mr. Dzik who was concentrating on stirring the batter again. "Four dogs to the front, please!"

The sheer amount of customers lining up didn't allot for me to write down the orders quickly enough on my little writing tablet. I began to make the cups of ice and added the lemonade, handing it to them to give Mr. Dzik time to complete the orders.

It was hectic but we were able to get all of the orders out in a timely fashion when Nicole showed up. I smiled at her while trying to keep everything professional. I didn't want Mr. Dzik to think I was messing around with friends while I was working.

"How are you holding up, Kimmy? I know you and Cindy were really close."

I did a double take and really looked at her, bewildered at her tone of voice. It looked like she had been crying. Her makeup was smeared and her clothes were wrinkled—nothing like the beauty queen I was used to seeing when she hung out with us.

"What are you talking about?" More people were beginning to line up behind her and she stepped aside.

"Excuse me, can I have a corndog please?" someone asked.

"Get the orders," my boss butted in, his first words to me all day. I continued taking orders and passing it along to Mr. Dzik, handing people their meals quickly without spilling their drinks on their trays.

"You mean to tell me you don't know?" Nicole said again as I filled another order. "No one told you?"

"Can I have a lemonade?" another person asked.

"Told me what?" I questioned as I took in another order. *This was beginning to feel a little strange.*

"It just doesn't feel real," she choked out and began to sob, wiping her eyes with the back of her hand, smearing more mascara down to her snotty nose.

This has to be something serious. She would never be caught dead looking this bad. When I finally got a reprieve from the customers, I took in a deep breath and fully turned to her. "What is going on? Tell me."

"Can you get the crying girl from the counter? She is detouring customers," Mr. Dzik growled. "Hey girl, this is a place of business! If you need therapy, call a therapist!"

I frowned and slapped his arm with the back of my hand. I was trying to listen to what she had to say! Mr. Dzik growled and shoved me toward her as he picked up where I left off with orders.

Her voice cracked while she continued to force out words through her sobs, hiccuping now and again. "Cindy went missing a while ago. She never came home," she finally got out, and my heart stopped. "She was in the truck with some guys and the truck has disappeared. The last person who saw them said they had all been drinking."

As she began to break down, my heart stuttered. My chest ached like a physical wound—a hole ripped from my chest. My eyes burned and suddenly my face was as wet as hers.

People who were close enough to hear us began to console her when my world started spinning. My mind replayed the last words we spoke to each other and now... *I would never get to see her again.*

I broke.

Everything became a haze.

I wasn't sure what happened but I came back to myself, sitting on a fold out chair at the back of The Good Char, my hat still on my head. My face was covered in tears and snot covered the back of my hands as I wiped my nose again, sniffling silently in my little corner.

Mr. Dzik was spraying disinfectant on the counter and mumbling to himself. I was at a loss at what occurred between hearing the news and me sitting here. Nicole's voice floated back to my head like it was on constant rewind and replay on my boombox. The memory slammed into me like a slap in the face.

Cindy was missing.

I bursted out with a new fresh set of hot tears.

"Are you crying *again*?" Mr. Dzik growled. "You already scared off customers, dripped snot on several corndogs for the past thirty minutes instead of working."

"I'm sorry," I sobbed louder. "It's-it's just, Cindy is gone. I may never see her again! And the last thing we did was fight!" I was feeling all kinds of emotions when I began to scream.

"Hey, calm down." Mr. Dzik brought his hands up, palms out in a placating manner with a grimace on his face. "You're stirring up the pigeons. I don't want them to fly in here and crap on my stuff. Are you listening to me? Breathe."

How was that even possible? We were inside a food court. He was so silly and knew exactly what to say to make me feel better. I stifled a laugh through my tears and he tilted his head.

Mr. Dzik was such a funny man. I got up from my seat, walked over and spontaneously wrapped my arms around him before breaking down again. I couldn't help it. He always stood by me like a strong pillar. I needed that strength now more than ever.

He awkwardly patted my shoulder but I couldn't hold it back anymore. I wanted to laugh, I wanted to cry. *I didn't know what I wanted.*

Yes, I do. I want Cindy back.

"If you're done leaking from your face, I need you to close shop," he said in a softer tone, his fingers still patting my back.

I gave him another squeeze and exhaled. He smelled nice. The hug made me feel better even though my heart still hurt.

"Okay," I replied softly, sniffling.

Mr. Dzik handed me a towel and pretended to look toward the food court. I smiled brightly at his thoughtfulness and blew snot into it. It was embarrassing that he had to see that, but it was better than not being able to breathe.

"Thank you, Mr. Dzik."

"Dzik," he said, clearing his throat gruffly. "Get back to work."

I threw away the towel and washed my hands to the sound of Mr. Dzik spraying disinfectant once more. We silently closed shop together and even with keeping my hands busy, my mind was still overwhelmed. I slowly walked to my bicycle and before I could reach for my helmet, someone took it from my hands from behind.

I turned to see Mr. Dzik in full concentration as his large fingers fiddled with the latch... right before he strapped it on my head.

We didn't say a word as my eyes began to mist again, staring at his strong, stubbled set jawline. When the helmet was secure, he lifted me up as if I weighed as much as a feather and placed me on my bicycle before turning and walking back to Hellscape Mall.

CHAPTER 17

MR. DZIK

She's smearing snot on my apron. I needed to remove her from me. I had never been hugged by a human before except for when they wanted to jump and attack me in the underworld, thinking it would stop the tortures.

This little human was visibly upset. She held me firmly in her deathly grasp with a strength I didn't know she could possess. I did the only thing I could to pacify the situation so she would release her grip on me—I mimicked her and patted her with as little contact as I could.

She still wouldn't let go. In fact, she gripped me tighter.

I was getting human all over me. If the master heard about this, my sentence in the human realm might be extended.

"There, there," I tried, audibly swallowing bile

before letting out the next set of words. "It's going to be okay, just let it all out."

I should give her the rest of the day off. I was tired of her leaky face. I didn't need any more of her minions coming by the counter with any other bad news.

I opened my mouth to tell her just that when she let out another sad sniffle. Something inside of my chest twinged. I didn't like what I was feeling. I didn't like any of this at all. It needed to stop and it needed to stop now.

"If you're done leaking from your face, I need you to close shop," I tried to tell her in a softer tone, one that wouldn't cause any more of these disgusting sounds. I patted my fingers on her back for emphasis and handed her a towel, anxious to disinfect the place once more to rid myself of her strange tumultuous emotions. For all I knew, it was contagious.

"Thank you, Mr. Dzik."

Why did this female insist on calling me with that title? I was a demon! *I am Dzik!* If she saw me in my true form she would cower in fear. The imagery made me feel much better.

"Dzik," I told her yet again, clearing my throat. Sadly, she didn't know I was a demon. To her, I was just her superior here on the human realm in this wretched corndog vendor. "Get back to work."

She unhooked me from her latch and wiped her eyes. It looked like she wanted to say something further but I purposely ignored her, pulling out the mop to clean up the mess near her chair.

She quietly worked beside me and I let out a sigh of relief. I expected her tomorrow without the snot and crying.

Something inside of my chest pulled at my internal organs as I watched her dejectedly walk out of the mall to her bicycle. I cursed myself and grumbled as I followed behind her to make sure there were no other surprises waiting. That would just be my luck. I needed her employment to remain sound. I didn't need any other accidents that would cause me to have to hire anyone new.

No one would compare after working with Kimmy. It was a horrible fact I was now stuck with.

I watched as her hands shook, reaching for her helmet and I bared my teeth in aggravation. Humans were frail. Weak. It was no wonder so many ended up in the underworld.

I quickly grabbed her helmet and placed it on her head, fiddling with the straps the way I had seen her do. What the blasted hell was this sorcery? Why were the clasps this tiny?

She stared at me with her large innocent eyes. My skin itched and I forced myself to work my fingers faster to get away from her. When the stupid latch finally clicked I wanted to roar in triumph. When her eyes began to mist, I inwardly groaned.

Not again.

Quickly lifting her onto her bicycle, I nudged

her along. She needed to keep on task and get herself home safely so that she would be able to come back to work bright and early tomorrow.

I quickly left her, unwilling to allow her disgusting emotions to cloud my own. I also needed to disinfect everything once more. *Who knows what kind of weird human diseases she or that other snotting girl left behind.*

I didn't need the health department to threaten to shut me down again. I was still paying that fucker off when he found the human finger that didn't get grinded down. I couldn't wait for his demise. Hopefully by the time they came back around, my sentence should be over and I would be able to torture him back in the underworld. I snickered aloud. Karma was very much a real thing, especially for him.

Thoughts of that blasted health department employee and Justin in the torture chambers lightened my mood enough for me to take off my apron, throw it with the dirty towels and change into new one.

I diligently cleaned the counters and sprayed disinfectant in the air before I started on my new germ free batter. I swear these humans were a plague on the earth. I didn't know how Obsideo dealt with it.

Thoughts of Kimmy's face melting made me grimace in both disgust and a tinge of something else I couldn't put my finger on. I scowled, concentrating. Trying to figure it out.

"Got crying employees now, huh. Why am I not surprised? And why are you closing so early, it's not even sundown yet," came the last voice I wanted to hear. I slowly raised my head up to find Justin with a smirk in front of my counter.

I pointed my gloved hand with the spray bottle right at his face and sprayed. The television said it worked for pesky felines, and it seemed to work with pesky humans as well. He sputtered comically and waved his hand in front of his face.

I cackled and sprayed again and again until he let out a bunch of expletives and finally left my sight back to his sickly sweet cave he passed off as sustenance.

After my laughter died down, I sighed. The entertainment was short lived. Another day in this fucking fairytale that I have been cursed to live in. A deep, low growl sounded off in the distance. I turned my gaze to the front of the mall, through the glass doors and up to the sky.

Ah, we were blessed to see the wondrous sight of dark clouds moving in. The day was turning for the better. *Finally some darkness. Now this is what I'm talking about!*

My spirits were fully uplifted at last. I bobbed my head to the low music in the mall, a heavier, electric guitar filled tune coming over the speakers. When my sentence was over, I was going to introduce some of the other demons to it so that it could be played along to the sounds of screams of agony.

Flashes of lighting brightened the room and I

smiled as I finished sanitizing The Good Char. It was the perfect background to go along with everything that had happened.

My happiness was interrupted by the sun peeking its eyes through the clouds, cutting through the beloved darkness like a hot knife through butter.

Just a little darkness, that's all I ask for. But, no. The sun had to shine. This punishment was becoming more than I could bear. Was it too much to get a small plague? Hell, I was sure Obsideo could give me some pointers when I returned home. A swarm of locusts, maybe a tsunami wave? Instead we got sunshine and happiness.

Groaning, I slammed my disinfectant down and sat myself on the same chair Kimmy was in earlier during her breakdown. Running a hand over my face, I titled my head back, staring at the ceiling. *Someone wake me up from this fairytale ending!*

I wanted to roar out in frustration when a group of kids came up to the closed counter after seeing me there.

"Hey, mister. We want some snow cones."

I snapped my head in their direction and my nostrils flared with agitation. It was him again. The kid with the red hair and freckles, and he had his flunkies with him this time.

When was this blasted sentence going to end? Everyday these brats come to my stand asking for snow cones and everyday I tell them, I didn't sell snow cones. *Okay, I got something for the little bastards.*

A menacing grin slowly stretched across my face.

"Okay, little boys," I purred before getting to my feet and making my way toward them. "What flavors would you like?"

"Um, we like red and blue mostly," the redhead leader said.

I leaned in and grinned wider. "That will be a dollar a piece. So, three dollars in total."

Each of them pulled a dollar from their fanny packs and handed it to me. I put the money into my cash register, made my way to the back of my kitchen, filled up three cups of ice and squirted some blue and red food coloring onto some pink lemonade and handed them the cups.

One of them frowned. "Hey! These aren't snow cones!" His tone was filled with indignation as he looked into his cup. The other boys looked as confused as he was.

"I know," I chuckled. "I don't sell snow cones but since you wanted some, I always stick to the moniker of the customer's always right. You three make sure to come back tomorrow now." *I hope you all wake up with boils.* "And we're closed for the day, so enjoy your snow cones." I cackled before leaving them standing there and making my way into the back room once again.

Little brats got what they deserved.

When I heard the sound of ice and liquid

hitting some of the equipment, I barreled out of the room to find the little shits laughing and running away, the cups left on the floor. Growling and shaking my fists at their retreating form, I memorized their faces for future reference when I was back in the underworld.

Nasty little ingrates. Quickly cleaning up the place once again, I throw my apron down and leave the area, walking out of the Hellscape Mall. I was done with human-ing. Done with them all.

Once outside, I let out a frustrated sigh and stretched my arms up. *What else could happen today?*

A man wearing a dark suit and carrying a thick, black book decided that he wanted to test his mortality around me, walking right in my direction with a smile on his face, bent on harassing me.

Why did I have to ask? I set myself up, didn't I? Or was this part of the master's punishment?

The stranger opened his mouth before I could tell him to go away. "Do you have a minute to talk about Revelations? The end of the world is coming, are you prepared? If you aren't, I have some pamphlets right here to help you be prepared for the end of days."

The fires lit within me. I was at my wits end. I looked at him with a menacing grin. "I hope it comes tomorrow. There's nothing like watching the flames of the underworld consume everything —including you!"

I let out a hysterical laugh, the madness

creeping in. It didn't matter anymore. None of it did.

His eyes grew as large as those sickly sweet rolls before he hurried away in the opposite direction from me, tripping on his own feet and scattering his pamphlets all over the parking lot.

I bit the air in threat but it wasn't like he could see me do it. That wasn't the point. The point was, I was done.

Why couldn't these humans just leave me be?

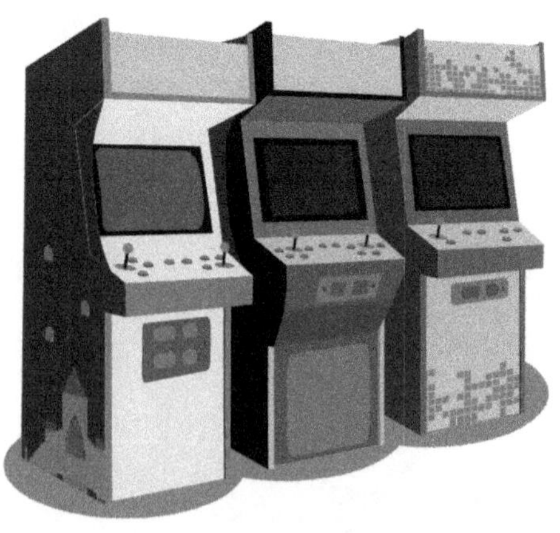

CHAPTER 18

KIMMY

I COULDN'T BELIEVE CINDY WAS MISSING. WHAT IF I never got to see her again? What if they never found her and the last thing we did was fight. I rode my bike as fast as I could to get to my parents' restaurant. *Maybe my parents could help me find her.*

I arrived at the back of the restaurant, located in another plaza, dropped my bike and ran through the back door. My heart was breaking with every step I took.

"Mom, Dad!" I sobbed while I walked through the kitchen where several of the workers were cleaning and prepping food for service. They looked at me, saw my current state and quickly got out of my way. My mother was the first to hear me and closed the distance between us.

She took one look at me and pulled me in for a tight hug. "What's wrong, Kimmy?"

My sobs got worse and I began hiccuping. It was hard for me to get the words out. She grabbed my hand and pulled me into their office for privacy.

"What happened? You *are* pregnant, aren't you? Sweetheart, it's okay, you can still live a great life as a single mom." She looked like she swallowed a live frog while she was trying her best to comfort me.

"Mom. Once again, for the hundredth time, I'm not pregnant!" I screamed through my sobs.

"Shhh, baby, listen to me. Our workers don't need to hear about your pregnancy, not right now. It's not that we are ashamed that you got yourself pregnant at such a young age," she lied, "but you have us, and we will get through it together as a family."

She rocked me back and forth, patting the back of my head, shoving my face against her chest.

Was she listening to anything I was saying?

"Mom!" I cried out, pushing against her forced comfort. This was not what I needed right now! "I'm not pregnant. Cindy went missing and they can't find her!"

My father came in just as new sobs bursted out. "What is the meaning of this, Margie? What did you say to her?"

"Harold, her friend Cindy went missing," she informed him before she gasped aloud, turning to me with knowing eyes and grabbed both of my hands. "You murdered her, didn't you? Baby, we need to get you out of the country right now! Harold, we have to fly her out tonight. Do the police suspect you in any way?"

What?!

My father quickly interjected with his fatherly logic. "No, Margie. If she killed someone's child she needs to turn herself in and do the right thing. Like I've always said, don't do something if you can't live with the consequences."

I watched, dumbstruck at the turn of conversation while my father began pacing around the office with his hands in his pockets.

How in the world did we get to this?

"Both of you, just please, stop! My friend is missing and you both are rambling on and on about nonsense." I bolted up and stared directly at them, wiping my wet face with the back of my hands. I was so mad, I couldn't even cry anymore. "I'm not pregnant. I didn't murder anyone. Gah! What is wrong with you two? And you wonder why I don't want to work here anymore!"

My heart raced at my tone of voice. I knew it was disrespectful but I couldn't contain it anymore. I left their office and the restaurant, getting back on my bike.

I'm going back to Mr. Dzik's place. At least he listens and understands me.

I pedaled as hard as I could back to The Good Char. I didn't know if he was there since he sent me home early but I was willing to try. I didn't have anywhere else to go or anyone else in my life now that Cin was gone.

When I finally made it back to the mall, our spot was closed. Growling in frustration, I stomped back out the mall and toward my bicycle. My hands were shaking from my anger that I couldn't snap my helmet off, causing me to consider throwing it on the ground. But I only had one helmet, and I needed to stay safe.

"What are you doing here?" came an overly gruff voice that sounded like he had been yelling. But to me, the voice made my body deflate in relief. He was here after all. "I gave you the day off."

I turned to find him walking toward me in all of his glory, his steps confident, his strength emanating off him like a visible aura. My lips trembled. I needed him. I needed him to keep me from falling into pieces.

"My parents are crazy! They think I killed Cindy and they keep asking me if I'm pregnant. I mean do I look pregnant to you?" I lifted my shirt up and showed him my flat stomach.

His eyes widened and his nostrils did that flaring thing again. He looked left and right as if searching for something then brought his gaze back to me, his hand rubbing the back of his neck. "No, you look like a normal girl to me."

I felt a set of fresh tears threatening to spill so I tilted my head back and tried to blink them away. How many times did I need to come to Mr. Dzik looking like a hot mess? He didn't deserve this. I was surprised he hadn't fired me.

I shouldn't be. He was too nice. That was why he hadn't fired me. I tried to take my helmet off again but my hand slipped as I removed it halfway and I gasped, anticipating it hitting the ground. Mr. Dzik arm shot out and he grabbed it before it could, placing it into my basket safely.

My breath stuttered. I felt like an utter failure. I hung my head in my hands and cried. "Why did Cindy have to go missing? She is my best friend. Why didn't I stop her from going with those guys? I knew something bad was going to happen. This is all my fault, isn't it?" I asked with a whisper.

Mr. Dzik grumbled before he pulled me in for a hug. I wrapped my arms around him and wiped my face against his black shirt. His body tensed but I held him tighter. After a few moments, he relaxed and began patting my back before rubbing it.

It felt nice and I turned my face to lay my head against his hard chest.

When he spoke, I could feel the deep vibration of his voice going through me. "No, this isn't your fault at all."

I let out a sigh. I shouldn't be enjoying his hugs this much. Wasn't this what my father always warned me of? His fear of my naivety leading me to latch onto the first man that gave me attention?

But it wasn't true. That boy the other day was trying to flirt with me and I felt nothing for him. This wasn't like that. This was so much different...

I felt comfort in his arms and found myself rubbing his back too. He didn't push me away. Instead, I think he pulled me closer and rearranged us so we would fit together better.

My face flushed and I wanted to giggle in nervousness but I bit my lip instead to hold it in. Who would have thought I'd be in the arms with an attractive bad boy like Mr. Dzik? When his hand ran to my lower back, something poked me from the front. My eyes bulged out. Was he...was he getting aroused by our proximity?

My entire body felt hot as embarrassment and intrigue coursed through me.

Wow, he was big. I mean, he was a big man in general, standing a few heads taller than me but he was *really* big.

When it twitched against me, we both kind of choked and coughed, scrambling to detangle from one another. When my hand accidentally grazed his crotch, I wanted to die. He let out a groan that made me press my legs together before quickly turning around and letting out some deep breaths.

Oh, my god. Oh my god! I discreetly fanned myself, trying to calm my nerves.

Okay, so I totally touched his junk and it grew. Did that mean he liked me?

Kimmy, he's your boss! What are you doing?

Mr. Dzik was constantly there for me and Cindy always said the best way to get over sadness was to get under happiness.

I didn't hear him leave. He continued to stand

there behind me. What should I do? Should I just go for it? I mean, there had always been a strange tension between us.

I was going to do it. Life is so short.

I felt him close the distance behind me so I spontaneously turned around, closed my eyes and tried to kiss him. But of course, it wasn't going to happen smoothly like the movies I love to watch. I twisted my legs and tripped on myself somehow, falling onto the floor hard with a loud thump.

I guess he moved! I'm such a spaz!

"Are you okay?" he asked with nonchalance, cool and collected. "You need to be careful. I don't want you breaking your bicycle."

I was too embarrassed to look at him. "Yes, Mr. Dzik, I'm fine," I lied through a grimace.

Nothing on my body hurt but my ego was crushed, shot down completely, and he pretended like nothing happened between us.

"Well," I laughed nervously, changing the subject quickly to save myself further embarrassment while dusting myself off. "One thing we should be able to agree on is we can thank God for the storm passing over. Look at how pretty it is. I was wondering if it was gonna storm today, but, just like I was hoping, the sun wins! Woohoo!"

I gave a little fist pump toward the sky like the dork I was.

"We are going to have a bright and sunshiny day, aren't we?" I concluded with a nervous giggle, looking up at the sky.

It was a beautiful day, even though Cindy was missing. Maybe she would turn up. In my heart, I hoped she would, trying to stay positive. They probably took a trip to the beach and here I am having a meltdown. I should be more grateful. I shouldn't think of all the worst case scenarios and work myself up. It was a sunny day and I have a job I love—and a guy I'm gushing over.

Today is a good day.

CHAPTER 19

DZIK

I inwardly growled. *No, not the G word*. Why was I continuously tortured by this little human female? Hadn't I been tortured enough, being forced to manage that wretched place? How long must I live a life of serving humans with no end in sight? There was only so much a demon could take and I was at my limit with all this goodness and happiness.

I needed death and destruction. Was that too much to ask?

Not only did this little female have the audacity to touch my phallus, she went as far as lifting her shirt up and showing me her flesh. Was this a human ritual of some sort? Was she asking to copulate? Her cackles were almost as bad as mine. *I did get a good glimpse of the underside of her bazookas though.* If she was performing some sort of court-ing, I had to say... they were impressive.

What the hell was I saying? Was I truly enter-taining the thought of copulating with a human? Haven't I had enough of them during my time here?

But there was something about Kimmy. She wasn't like the other imbeciles.

I narrowed my eyes in concentration as she continued to babble on, distracted by the sun in the sky. She was simple, I'd give her that. Perhaps that was what made her so intriguing. Pashar was another demon in the human realm I came across during my sentence at the Hellscape Mall. He manned the Dark Spells Comic book store. He'd surely have access to a manual about fucking humans.

I didn't remember if fornication was punish-able or not. I rubbed the scruff of my face as I continued to watch her animatedly talk about some bullcrap or another. I wasn't listening, but I did enjoy looking at her face the longer I was around her.

She was definitely hard working. It was an admirable trait, one that was rare among the idiots that walked the mall. She would be perfect if she wasn't so happy all the time and randomly leaked from her face at odd moments.

If I could just get her to shut her damn mouth.

"Kimmy."

She kept babbling and I scowled.

"Kimmy," I tried again to no avail.

"Blasted hell woman!" I roared, grabbing her by the waist and placing her against my side as I dragged her back into the mall through another entrance and to the back room of The Good Char. Placing her back on her feet, she looked at me stunned with her mouth in a little 'o'.

It shouldn't be as enticing as it looked. Her shutting up probably played a good part in why my hands landed on her shoulder, pulling her into me and my lips slamming on hers.

My hands squeezed her shoulders every so often, unsure of where they should be. I'd never kissed a human before but her lips were decadent against my own, hesitantly moving against mine.

The smell of her fear and lust made something grow inside of me. I enjoyed the fact that her little hands crawled along my shoulders, wrapping themselves around me as if I was the only thing that kept her from sliding onto the floor.

She let out a soft sigh and my cock strained further against my pants, wanting to make its claim right then and there. Surely we wouldn't fit. She was so tiny. My phallus would break her in two.

Wouldn't you like to see and feel that anyway, you debauched demon, you?

When her tongue entered my mouth, I groaned, lost in whatever witchcraft she was weaving over me. My mind began thinking about the consequences—*blasted hell, fuck the conse-quences.*

I playfully nipped at her lip as my tongue sparred with hers. She closed whatever small distance remained between us and my cock slapped against her through the fabric of my pants. She giggled and for once it wasn't annoying me.

The more passionately she kissed me, the more I felt my flesh suit begin to strain against the expansion of my true form. I could feel the phantom sensation of my tail wagging back and forth and my horns itching against my scalp.

When her hand slid down the front of my pants and began rubbing in a circular motion, I almost ripped out of my skin. I kissed her jaw to give myself a chance to collect myself, breathing in her scent, memorizing it until my body finally calmed enough to continue.

I didn't know who this female was in front of me when her little hands grabbed my face and forced our lips together once more. The intensity of our kiss amplified to infernal heights. Everything around us became nonexistent as I let the little vixen guide me whatever way she wanted as long as she didn't stop.

Was this why so many demons found them-selves not wanting to return home after elongated periods in the realm of men? I didn't blame them. *I didn't know it could be like this.*

I was completely lost in the moment when her hand performed some sort of demonry and made me unanticipatedly release in my pants. My eyes snapped open in utter surprise.

Fuck! I can't believe I just did that. How is that possible? I hope she didn't notice. I grimaced when I felt her wipe her hand on the back of my pants.

Blasted hellfires.

She broke the kiss and pulled away from me, looking at me from beneath her hooded lashes. What was this? Who was this woman? I felt the phantom sensation of my tail whipping again, but this time in agitation.

"I-it's okay, you know. It's alright. I hope that helps you from being Mr. Grumpy," she giggled.

My flesh suit threatened to rip again. A growl escaped and her eyes widened with a sparkle. My nostrils flared as I took in her scent again, one that was surrounding me, seeped into my clothes.

I wanted her.

Despite feeling better from my release, as she put it, my mind continued to wonder where the hell I put that damn manual?

It was a prank gift from the other demons upon the first day of my sentence, sent with the initial crate of human meat. It was a hand scribed tome that dictated what I could and couldn't do as a demon while on probation in the human realm.

This situation with Kimmy was precarious. I desperately needed its guidance now. But I couldn't let her know I was a demon. Not yet. I left her standing there as I found a rag and cleaned myself up in the backroom. I hadn't had a release like that in centuries and my cock continued to strain against the fabric of my pants even after I resituated things.

This was going to be a problem. A big problem. And a demon like me, didn't need any more problems.

I returned to the main area to find her still standing there, with her hands innocently clasped in front of her as if she didn't just try to pull my soul out of my cock with her bare hands.

"Kimmy." I cleared my throat and straightened myself in front of her. She needed to understand who was in control here and who was the servant. "What just happened, can't happen again. You're my employee and we have to keep this a business relationship."

I was talking out of my ass and I knew it. I very much wanted her little hands on me again and her lips. I began to fantasize about what it would feel like to have her lips where her hands were...

"And I don't want to take advantage of your grief," I gritted out, frustration leaking through my voice.

A wicked smile crossed her face and a tinge of fear coursed through me. I took a step back, watching her closely. She truly was sent here to torture me. *The best and worst kind of torture.* I scowled, trying to right the order of things between us.

"You aren't taking advantage of me," she purred. Where did she learn how to purr like that?

"But I understand," she continued solemnly. "From now on, it's strictly professional Mr. Dzik, and I'm sorry for getting out of line."

I was annoyed. I wasn't sure if it was from the way she quickly brushed it off and followed my command or the way she initially purred her response to me.

My emotions and thoughts were in a jumble and that only further agitated me in my current state of being. We both stood there awkwardly. I crossed my arms and she watched the way my body flexed, making me puff out my chest in response.

I chastised myself. This had to end. This couldn't happen between us. The demons back home were setting me up. I turned away and randomly began cleaning the counter top.

"Well, if you're going to be here. Get back to work!" I barked.

She laughed softly and began sweeping.

CHAPTER 20

KIMMY

A FEW PAYCHECKS IN AND MY LITTLE APARTMENT WAS furnished enough for me to stay.

"My own place. I can't believe I did it," I whispered, looking around the plain walls with a big smile.

It was still somewhat sparse, but I had a bed, the lower box that sat on the floor, a loveseat and a kitchen table. I would need to grab a microwave next and maybe a few pots and pans.

Nodding my head, I left my apartment, intent on checking my mail. Turning my key to lock the door, I lifted my eyes to see my strange neighbor down the hall looking at me again. I waved and he tipped his head. We never spoke but he seemed friendly.

Shrugging my shoulders, I went down a couple flights of stairs to the mailroom. Humming to myself, I unlocked my box and took out the few letters that were in it. My heart stuttered. The first was a bill.

Did I miss one? I could have sworn I calculated and paid everything on time. I could have sworn!

"Please, please, please," I chanted, hoping that it would say zero dollars.

I ripped it open and slowly pulled it out and felt my eyes burning from tears forming.

"Oh, good, they fixed the mailboxes. Whoever was stealing mail won't be able to do it now," came an unfamiliar voice beside me. I blinked a few times and turned to look at them. It was an older woman who probably also resided in the apartments. "You must be new, I haven't seen your face around. Welcome. Why would a pretty girl like you decide to live in a dump like this?"

I sniffed and shrugged my shoulders, at a loss for words. My mind was still reeling over the fact that my utility bill was doubled, stating that a payment was missed.

It was nice of our landlord to fix our mailboxes. But it didn't change the fact that I was left with the repercussions. How in the world was I going to pay this on time? I wasn't even sure if my next paycheck would cover it all.

I felt defeated. I would have to stay with my parents a bit longer. It was the only way I could save. Keeping the lights off in my apartment made a big difference. I had yet to turn on the water, trying to hold that off for last. And I still needed to purchase cookware. So it was either scrounge up money quickly to pay this bill, or not be able to have any tools to make food. Maybe I could ask Mr. Dzik for more hours somehow.

"Well, see you around!" my neighbor waved as she turned and walked back to her apartment with her cane and mail in hand.

I shoved the rest of the mail into my hoodie pocket and made my way to my bicycle. Mr. Dzik gave me the day off with full pay, mumbling something about needing distance.

Well, this was an emergency so he was going to have to suck it up and see me again. The trip was quick, my mind occupied the entire time. Parking my bike, I took off my helmet and fluffed my hair out before tying it into a ponytail. Marching to the food court, I beelined straight to The Good Char with my eyes glued on his form.

As if he could sense me, he snapped his head up and shoved the order in his hand into the customer's chest.

"Hey! Watch it!" the poor guy whined.

"Get out," he snapped.

"Rude!"

Mr. Dzik turned his head toward the man and the man scrambled away with his corndog.

"Mr. Dzik—" I started, prepared with a full eloquent speech inside my head.

"Dzik," he glared and I suddenly lost my confidence.

Come on, Kimmy. You can do this.

"Can you give me more hours? I need the extra money. Something came up and it would really help get me out of a bind. Not that it matters to you but if you could help me out, I would greatly appreciate it. Please."

I finally took a breath. Not at all what I prepared but close enough to get my desperation across.

"What kind of bind?" he grunted. He didn't seem happy. Oh no. Please, please!

"I-Something happened that was out of my control and now I have to find a way to fix it. I spent the last paycheck on a couch for my apartment, you know, so I don't have to sit on the floor anymore and I don't think I'll have enough to do this thing that I have to do..."

I sounded idiotic even to my own ears.

"So you want to... work more, is this what I'm hearing?"

I nodded frantically. "I appreciate you always giving me time off, please don't think otherwise. I just need this so desperately, please. It would help me so much, Mr—er, Dzik."

Giving him a bright smile, he frowned and grunted before turning and walking toward the back room.

"Hey! Can I get some service here?" came a woman's voice behind me. "How rude! He saw me standing here this whole time!"

"I'll help you. Just give me a second," I told her. Quickly getting behind the counter, I got her order and rang her up. "Here's a free lemonade. Sorry about that."

"Thank you. You're one of the only reasons why I keep coming back here. The other guy is a jerk."

I laughed nervously and gave her a bright smile. "Thank you, come back soon!" I waved.

"What are you doing?" my boss barked behind me and I shrank in place.

"Helping out?" I squeaked, biting my lip and turning toward him.

"I told you to take the day off! Here," he shoved an envelope toward me, making sure not to make any contact.

He was acting like a toddler. Why were boys so weird? I purposely touched his fingers as I took it from him and his nostrils flared but he didn't look away.

"Take it and leave," he said with finality.

"What about more hours?"

"Leave, Kimmy. Now!" he roared and I jumped and did as he commanded, not looking back until I made it to my bicycle. Gosh, he really was extra grumpy today. One would think helping him relieve himself the other day would make his mood better. Apparently not.

Or maybe he was so pent up, one wasn't enough. Hmm. Good point, Kimmy. Don't give up on the guy yet. He needs you.

Nodding my head to my own internal dialogue, I opened the envelope and pulled out my paycheck. I almost dropped it. My eyes blurred quickly from the tears as I brought my hand to my mouth.

I ran back inside, straight to The Good Char. Parting everyone around me, I made my way behind the counter and tackled my boss with a hug, wrapping my arms around his shoulders.

He tensed up and growled beside my ear but a few moments later, I felt his arms wrap around me too.

"Thank you, Mr. Dzik. Thank you so much. You didn't have to," I whispered, choking at the end.

"Everyone leave. The Good Char is closed for the rest of the day," he bit out, never letting me go.

"What? I've been standing here for like—"

Dzik lifted me and turned to face the man.

"Sorry. Sorry. I'm going," the man mumbled and I giggled.

"What's so funny?" he snarled at me, his hand rubbing my lower back softly.

"You, grumpy pants. You."

He groaned and put me back on my feet. "Don't make me tell you again, Kimmy. Leave. You're off today. I don't want to see you back and I definitely do not need any conversations about pants with you. Go!"

"Yes, sir!" I saluted, right before I jumped up and gave him a peck on the cheek.

Dzik gave me more than enough to cover my late bill and then some. He had a heart of gold whether he wanted to admit it or not. It was little moments like these where I knew I was no longer the naive girl I was. Being around Dzik grounded me into reality and where I once saw the world through rose colored lenses, he helped remind me that it wasn't always that way... but he was there to catch me anyway when I didn't know I was falling.

He growled as I skipped away, feeling light on my feet, knowing that my dream at being independent was at my fingertips.

CHAPTER 21

DZIK

She thought she could keep her secrets from me.

As I stood there, in the shadows, watching her flit around her little apartment, I curled my lip at the dilapidated neighborhood and its location. How this place wasn't scheduled for demolition years ago was beyond my understanding.

I had been checking in on her for the past few weeks. Human authorities would call it stalking, I called it making sure my damn employee made it to work alive.

She only recently started visiting more often instead of veering back toward her parent's home in the nice suburbs. I didn't pretend to know what was going on in that little pretty head of hers but I knew one thing, she wouldn't make it without me.

Hell, just the other day I stumbled upon a bastard messing with the communal mailbox while I was getting a closer look at her little hell hole she called a residence. I made quick work of him, weeks of frustration pouring out of me as I choked him unconscious, dragged him out into a more secluded area and began clawing his skin until I reached tendons and muscles. Lost in the euphoria of torture, my flesh suit ripped and once I was done bathing in his blood, I had to sneak back into the underworld, dragging him with me.

Melkgard scowled and complained that I had dirtied the meat but it didn't matter. Because it seemed I gave Daniel a companion for his stay.

Watching her light turn off, I grunted and straightened from leaning against my Camaro. This time around, there weren't any further distractions as I made my way inside the building, taking more of the visual atrocity in. It was evident whoever ran the place pocketed all the money.

I wouldn't be surprised if the master planted another demon here.

The scuff of a shoe had me turning to find a man down the hall from Kimmy's apartment, staring at me for a few seconds before he disappeared into his own hell hole.

Peculiar, but not my damn problem.

I had curated a copy of the key to Kimmy's place and quietly unlocked her door and made my way inside. The sound of light snores floated in the air as I walked a few more steps to find her sleeping soundly on a mattress and box spring that sat directly on the floor.

How she found it within her to come to work as bubbly as she did nonplussed me. Or perhaps she was delusional from lack of sleep and appropriate sustenance—that would make more sense.

Standing at the foot of her bed, I watched her breathe.

It was nice not hearing her blabbering a million miles a minute, something I had come to learn was a reaction to her worries, frustration and nervousness.

Taking a few steps forward, I leaned down and stared at her relaxed face—one I came to expect everyday.

"Who are you, Kimmy Ngo?" I whispered as I inadvertently took in her scent again. The musk was lighter... until she turned and slapped me in the face.

Gritting my teeth, I cursed her under my breath as I shook my head.

"No, of course I'll get you a corndog!" she giggled then drifted back into silence.

Seemed the tortures of The Good Char haunted us both. Something we had in common.

Looking out her clouded window, I flicked my gaze to her one last time before leaving. The halls were quiet as I went down the couple flights of stairs, creaking the metal with each step.

Before I could fully exit the building, something pulled me back. I looked over my shoulder and grumbled about worthless employees before forcing myself to leave. This unwanted attachment was the bane of my existence. Scowling, I removed myself completely before something else pissed me off.

"Piece of crap apartment. How the hell am I supposed to keep up maintenance when crap keeps going out in every damn place?" came a growl from behind the shadows of the building.

My ears perked.

"I should just let this place burn to the ground, tenants and all."

My nostrils flared at his last statement and I stomped over toward his location, grabbing the scruff of his shirt before he was aware of my presence and slammed him against the wall.

"What did you say?" I snarled in his face.

"Who the hell are you? Put me down this instant!"

The desire for death and destruction grew within me like living fire. He dared to threaten to burn my employee where she slept soundly? My fangs grew as I gave him a menacing grin.

"Oh, I'll put you down alright. Straight into hellfire."

My claws ripped through my fingertips, piercing the flesh of his chest. His cry of agony was music to my ears, relinquishing me of the mix of emotions I left with.

"I'm sorry. I'm sorry. Please, don't hurt me!"

"Did you want to burn with them? Because I assure you, I can make that happen. I'll even send you to an after party with a few demons back home," I taunted.

Light chitter chatters floated around us, the sprites having caught on to our little game in the shadows. No one threatened what was mine.

Mine?

I scowled at memories of Kimmy's arms around me, making my phallus slap against the fabric of my pants.

"Wh-What do you want from me? I'll give you anything. Just please, don't hurt me!" he whimpered like the pathetic creature he was.

Disgusted with this pitiful human I dropped him to the ground and brought my boot against his chest to keep him there.

"Anything, you say?"

"Y-yes. Please," he begged right before the harsh smell of urine invaded my nose.

I was going to have to disinfect my boots after this encounter. Disgusting creature. A thought struck me and I snapped my fangs in his direction.

"You're going to give me an apartment."

"I am?" he asked, befuddled.

"Yes, you fool!"

"But there aren't any vacant—"

I pushed my foot down until it crunched. He cried out in a higher pitch and grabbed my ankle.

"Okay!" he squeaked and I nodded, removing my boot and wiping it on the grass beside him.

"Have it ready for me by tomorrow," I

commanded before returning to my Camaro with a new purpose.

I ignored the sounds of sprites as they appeared behind me, continuing to wreak havoc on him as he ran back into the building.

Hopefully, tales of my deeds in the realm of men didn't return with them once they went back to the underworld. I frowned at what Zychor and Belchar would say about what transpired here. They didn't understand what I had to deal with during my sentence. They never would.

Hell, they should be happy I was adding souls back home.

"I should have killed him," I grumbled as I started the car. But I didn't know the ins and outs of how to maintain a building if he went missing. I didn't need a miserable Kimmy coming to work or worse yet, not coming at all.

This was getting more complicated than I anticipated.

The blasted little human, what was she doing to me?

CHAPTER 22

KIMMY

As I sat here getting berated by my parents, I reminded myself as to why I was doing what I was doing.

I was a full grown woman, getting lectured about curfews. I understood that they were scared for my safety because I hadn't been away from home most of my life. Sleepovers were rare in itself since we worked so much at the restaurant.

But wasn't that the perfect reason why I needed to break from this cycle? Were my own children destined to forever be a part of this restaurant legacy? Sure, sleeping in my apartment alone for the first time was laced with some fear, but I kept a knife under my pillow just in case.

How was I supposed to stretch my wings like this?

"Kimmy! Are you listening? How could you

scare us like that?" my mother whined before she plopped down on the kitchen chair dramatically with her head hung in her hands.

I quietly looked at my father, who was fuming in silence with his hands clasped behind him. He shook his head and turned away from me, facing the outside window.

It was always going to be this way. Maybe because I was a younger generation thrown into western assimilation harder than they were, but with my first taste of independence, I was no longer the girl they knew.

I was no longer a girl. I was a woman and they needed to understand that. I just didn't know how to fully explain my reasoning without sounding like I was retaliating or being disrespectful for disrespect's sake.

"Mother, Father, I'm sorry. You won't understand it, but I need to do this. For me, for us. Please, just trust me," I tried.

The weight of their disapproval weighed heavily on my shoulders and old feelings of obligation and duty threatened to choke me, but I sat there with a soft smile, trying to keep calm.

"I need to go to work. My shift starts soon," I whispered before getting to my feet.

"Have you been staying with him? Was that why you were gone last night?" My father finally spoke without turning around.

"You're pregnant. I knew it. You're farther along and you're trying to hide your belly from us.

You don't need to live under his rule, Kimmy. You can still stay with us." my mother sniffed.

I let out a sigh. "I'm not pregnant. There's just a lot that's been going on in my head and I need to figure things out on my own. You understand that, don't you? You guys came here and started a new life. I'm just doing the same in my own way. It's time. I'm going to be in my mid twenties soon enough. I can't stay with my parents forever," I explained.

My mother bawled while my father turned to look at me seriously before pacing. "Why are you trying to leave me?"

"I'm not leaving forever. I just won't be living here. I need to get out on my own. I'm sorry." I blinked back a few of my tears as I ran up the stairs and grabbed a backpack, stuffing more clothes in it and a few pictures of my family.

Avoiding their faces, I quickly made my way to my bicycle and pedaled as fast as I could, letting the wind erase my sadness and the sun replace my happiness as I weaved through the suburbs toward Hellscape Mall.

By the time I made it to the mall's plaza, cars were filling up and I had to carefully ride to the sidewalk, then walk the rest of the way.

"Today is going to be a good day. The sun is shining. My first night at the apartment went okay. Besides the weird argument outside my window, I thought it went pretty well," I talked to myself as I walked through the glass doors.

The air conditioning hit me in the face and I let out a relieved sigh. Who would have thought a trip to the mall would be uplifting? It was sad that my parents home was now something I cringed about.

The food court wasn't bustling yet as I waved at some of the other employees who were setting up.

I watched my boss' back as he worked on the batter, never once turning when I made my way behind the counter.

"Good morning, Mr. Dzik," I greeted him as I grabbed my apron and hat.

He grunted in response before peeking at me through the side of his eye.

I chuckled. "What?"

He grunted again, moved the batter, turned on the fryer and the grill.

I wrapped my hair in a loose bun, ignoring his grumpy attitude like usual before manning the register. Leaning over the counter, I looked out the glass doors of the front of the mall and smiled brightly.

I had a good feeling about today despite how it started. The duality within me was caught between old fashioned cultural upbringing and new generation liberation. Being raised to think of the collective whole will never fully leave me, but ideals of individualism were slowly starting to creep in and my parents couldn't blame me for the influences of our lives here in Nevada.

"Mr. Dzik—"

"Dzik," he grumbled.

"Dzik, do you live far from here? I don't think I've ever had the chance to see you come or go. Every time I arrive and leave, you're always just here at The Good Char." Turning my attention toward him, I gave him a mischievous smile. "You don't sleep in the back room do you? There are no showers and you don't stink."

I scrunched my nose playfully and I could have sworn I saw the corner of his lip twitch. It sparked something inside of me and suddenly I was determined to make the man smile.

"Do you have any pets?" I tried again, attempting to find a good opening to pry into his life like the nosy person I was. Well, I wasn't—only for him. Who was this mysterious bad boy? I watched his tattoos flex with his arm as he began spraying the counter and wiping it down more aggressively than necessary.

"I don't have time for that nonsense."

I slid over and leaned in, blocking his wiping path while looking up at him.

"Is it nonsense, Mr. Dzik? Pets are great! They're so cute and cuddly. When I see one I just want to pinch their cheeks so bad," I explained as I pushed my face together, making my lips pout comically.

He scowled and I crossed my eyes. His only response was to glare and I bursted out laughing.

"Mr. Dzik, you are one funny man. Why are you like this?"

"What are you talking about?" he gritted. "Move, I'm trying to clean."

"Make me," I challenged, straightening with my hands on my hips.

His nostrils flared and my eyes widened when my body perked up. I didn't know what it was about him that would elicit such a reaction to me but here we were, standing face to face awkwardly as my breath slowly came out in pants.

Pants.

I gulped. The other day's incident flashed before my eyes and I whimpered, pressing my legs together. Embarrassingly, his eyes darkened as if he thought the same right before he flicked his gaze down to the exposed skin of my collar.

"Are you challenging me, Kimmy? Are you challenging your boss?" he let out huskily and my nipples perked behind my shirt.

"M-Maybe I am. Would that get me in trouble?"

I wanted it to be a rhetorical question but it slipped through my lips and now I was afraid of the answer.

He took another step forward, mindlessly wiping the counter with one hand while keeping his eyes on me.

"You, little human, have been nothing but trouble from the moment I met you."

I didn't know how to take his nonchalant tone. Was there an underlying message here because I wasn't sure if this was a good or bad thing.

"I-Is that a bad thing?" I couldn't help but ask, biting my bottom lip.

"It's the worse thing—"

"Um, should I, like, come back later or…" came a stranger's voice.

I squeaked and jumped away from Mr. Dzik's scrutiny, placing my hands on my cheeks to cool them down. "I'm sorry. I hope you weren't standing there long. What would you like?"

The teenage boy looked between me and my boss, his own face flaming as he mumbled his order before fidgeting in place, waiting for it to arrive.

With a grunt, Mr. Dzik went to the fryer and threw a corndog in.

I let out a nervous laugh to break the tension. "You're our first customer of the day! Lucky you. We make our corndogs fresh to order. Have you been here before? Don't forget to tell your friends about us! We open a little before lunch until the mall closes."

"Yeah… I know," he replied apprehensively when Dzik stood beside me and handed him his order with a glare. The poor kid audibly swallowed and ran away to the farthest table from The Good Char.

"He was a nice boy wasn't he? We probably should throw a few more corndogs in, you know, in preparation for the lunch rush. Boys like him always hang out in groups and they eat a lot at that age," I rambled.

"Why do you know so much about boys, Kimmy?" he growled and I blinked a few times, taken aback by his strange question.

"I-I don't? I mean, these are things everyone knows, right?"

He narrowed his eyes and I could see the vein on his temple pulse. Why did it look so hot?

I opened my mouth to blabber about something else when another customer called for my attention. Phew!

"Hi there! Welcome to The Good Char! How may I help you?" I let out brightly.

A warm breath caressed the nape of my neck and my eyes fluttered. "This conversation is far from over, Kimmy."

CHAPTER 23

DZIK

I closed The Good Char the moment she left work and rode off on her bicycle.

"Where do you think you're going? Closing sporadically as much as you do, I'm surprised you're still in business, Dick," Justin called out from his side, his blue apron burning into my skull.

"Mind your business," I grumbled.

"The same way you mind yours?" he pointed his tongs at me menacingly, leaning his thin frame in my direction from behind his counter. "Don't think I forgot what you did to me. And I hired two new employees."

"Good for you. Now, stop talking to me." I turned off the neon sign, removed my apron and threw it on the back counter, heading toward the mall's exit.

"Hey! You know there are rules to abide by!" Justin called out. "If there's something iffy back there, don't think I won't call the health department on you."

I back stiffened and in the next few seconds I found my hand fisting the front of his shirt, lifting him off his feet. He squealed like a dying pig when I bared my teeth in his face.

"Would you like to say that again, Justin?" I enunciated, ready to send him to see my former employee in the underworld.

"Y-You can't threaten me. That's a crime. I'll call the cops!"

I slammed his head on his counter and growled beside his ear. "You go ahead and do that, Justin. I'll make sure the only thing they find is your corpse stuffed with baked goods and a sign that says 'thank you, come again', do you understand?"

He shook and I slammed his head again, causing some of the remaining patrons to run away screaming. It was a slow weekday, so not too many stragglers hung around past dinner time.

"I'm not going to repeat myself," I growled and he whimpered. Agreeing. "Good. Now that we have a clear understanding of each other, good luck with your new employees. Good ones are hard to come by. Tell me, did the other two get fired or did they go missing?"

I cackled as I tossed him back into his bay and walked away, uncaring of what his response was.

Was it a bluff? He would never know because I was done wasting my breath on a knucklehead sugar pusher like Justin fucking Reid.

Getting in my Camaro, I drove the familiar roads toward her apartment.

Our apartment.

A grin split my face when I saw her little bicycle parked outside. I slowly got out and went toward my bottom level apartment. The jackass landlord secured me an ideal location that was directly below hers with just a single floor separating us.

Grunting, I got out my key and ignored everyone around me who was staring. Once inside, I slammed the door and looked around the empty space. I discovered a secret latch in the middle of the floor, covered by a throw rug the moment I acquired this piece of crap home.

Curiosity had me exploring to find a small crawl space. I had been digging each night when Kimmy's face and phantom touches haunted me. The physical labor and pain in my muscles helped rid me of her temporarily and much to my delight... I stumbled upon stacks of skeletons beneath the building.

The interesting discovery had me digging further until an entire room was clawed out to my liking.

It smelled of death and decay. It reminded me of home.

Crawling into my personal hell hole, I climb

down onto a couch I hauled in. It was a horrendous feat to get inside, but I managed with a few scruffs and tears. Not that it mattered. It wasn't like I was trying to get my humble abode on television.

Chitter chatters of sprites was my first warning. I groaned when the rest of their voices came afterward.

"So this is where you're staying, Dick? Nice, nice. Not too bad," Zychor called out, kicking one of the sprites out of the way and slamming him into the cavern wall.

The disgusting splat, followed by a sulfuric smelling evaporation made me grin as I crossed my leg and rested my head against my closed fist.

His long tongue snaked out as if to test the air right as Belchar appeared.

"Well, well. Does the master know you're living it up here in the human realm? I almost feel cheated looking at this place here. Peace, quiet, solitude. And you don't have to look at Zychor's ugly face."

Zychor threw a punch and Belchar ducked, throwing a sprite in his place. Blood splattered on the walls and they both threw their heads back laughing at one another.

"Just like home," Zychor grinned. "What is that revolting thing you're sitting on, Dick?"

I scowled at his constant use of the stupid nickname. He reminded me too much of Justin. One of these days, Zychor was going to get what was coming to him. When his curved horns hit the ceiling, a cloud of dust fell on our heads and we all coughed, waving our hands in front of us.

"Would you watch where you're going, you fool?" I snarled.

"It's not my fault your pathetic little home can't accommodate an amazing demon like me," he growled back, jerking his head until more dust came down and he finally ripped his horns free.

"Enough about your small cock, Zychor. Why are you sitting on something that looks like an ancient human threw up?" Belchar spat out before sniffing around and plopping himself down beside me.

"Then why is your ass on it if it's so ugly? It's not uglier than the womb you came from," I taunted and Belchar snarled, ripping more of the fabric and cackling.

"Ah, that was a good one. When is your sentence over?"

Zychor scoffed. "When the master feels like it. Or when he kills off another demon in his rage. It would be easier for him to replace a demon with one he already knows than one he needs to find."

His long tongue snaked out and I wanted to tear it from his mouth. I didn't come here to hear them talk about my never ending sentence in this wretched place. My mind would like to think my sentence was coming to an end sometime this century, but with each day that passes the hope I harbored rotted. I could practically feel the maggots crawling all over it as we spoke.

"Why are you both here?" I barked out, irritation furling in my gut.

"What is this, Dick? Are you eating fresh human flesh in your off time? Why are there so many bones about?" asked Zychor curiously. His tone of voice sounded as if he was upset he wasn't invited if it were the truth.

I gave him a side eye and he scowled back.

"How am I supposed to know what humans are up to?" I snapped.

"Come on, Dick. You mean to tell me, you didn't choose this place *because* of this?" Belchar taunted, his beast-like face panting with his tongue lolled out while his tusks and half sloughed off skin shakes with his laughter. "I mean, by the looks of it, I'm surprised your gut hasn't exploded. That's a lot of bones, Dick."

I shoved him off my dirty floral couch with a growl. He landed in a heap, his horns hooking into the ground as sprites poofed in and began dancing on top of him, cackling with mirth.

"Good to see you haven't lost too much of yourself while you're here, Dick. Humans and their strange ways can be infectious. Look at Obsideo. He was gone so long, he came back with one," Zychor chuckled.

I rolled my eyes and clasped my hands behind my head, staring at the dirt ceiling. "Why are you guys here? You've never visited me before. Why now?"

"Ah, well," Zychor began, rubbing his distorted skull and jawline. "It was getting boring down there without you, torturing the same souls over and over again. They never seem to remember my taunts after they die and come back. Then I find myself throwing out the same taunts, eliciting the same response. It's monotonous over the eons. Was hoping for another plague to bring in fresh souls, but here we are... not a plague in sight since the last one."

"Zychor's memory is shit. We've had a small influx lately but they come one at a time much more frequently, sometimes two at a time. But he's right. It's not enough for entertainment. They all start to sound the same when they scream," chimed in Belchar as he ripped apart the closest sprite and bit into him.

"Your complaints are not my problem. My problem is your sorry asses taking up space in my domain. You both need to leave." Glaring at them, they both curled their lips before gnashing their teeth. I stared on without expression, waiting for them to do as commanded.

"Make sure you continue to feed and corrupt the humans up here, Dick. It's all you're good for these days," spat Zychor, a hint of jealousy still tinging his tone.

When I didn't respond, they both grumbled and ripped open a portal back to the underworld.

A wayward chitter chatter came behind my ear and I shot my arm out, grabbing the sprite and hurling him toward the other two idiots right before the portal closed on the sprite's tail, leaving it wriggling behind on the ground with a trail of blood.

CHAPTER 24

I PROWLED AROUND THE APARTMENTS WHILE THE WORLD was still asleep. The darkness called to me like a lover as I made my way up the steps toward her floor.

The scuffle of a shoe stopped me in my tracks as my eyes darted to its origins. He couldn't see me, but I could see him.

The man across the hall pulled in another figure quickly behind his door. A few thuds sounded as I continued my way toward Kimmy's door. It was just as sparse as I remembered. Hadn't I given her enough funds lately? I might need to adjust her pay again.

Frowning at her empty space, I looked at her little table with a single chair and her sheer curtains with the moonlight's glow.

She stirred in her sleep and I wondered what she was dreaming about.

Pfft. Why should I care what she dreams about

at all? She was merely my human servant here while I was serving my sentence—

A moan escaped her lips... and then my name. My back tensed and my phallus twitched. I grunted and took a few more steps beside her bed and watched her face contort through different emotions.

When she frowned, bit her bottom lip and turned over with her hair splayed behind her, I couldn't resist the pull. Leaning in, I slowly crawled onto her bed with one knee, and sniffed.

What was it about Kimmy that made her different from the rest of the population?

"Please, sir. Please..." she begged sweetly and my hackles rose. Who was she dreaming about? She wasn't calling out to me like that when my name left her lips. Anger began to flame but was quickly put out when her hand crawled between her legs and she whispered, "I can't call you D. Please don't make me, sir."

Her feminine musk cloaked the air and the next thing I knew, I was spooned behind her, my tail ripping through my flesh suit, thrashing back and forth over the edge. When she hummed, I felt the vibration against my skin and I pulled her closer against me, glad she wasn't awake to witness my weakness.

"Please," she begged again and I groaned, wrapping my hand around hers, wondering what her naughty little fingers were doing.

She squirmed against me and I growled as my

hardened phallus nested against her backside. "What are you begging for, little human?"

She whimpered as I guided her hands further between the apex of her legs, moving her fingers into steady teasing motions. Her breath stuttered as her pheromones grew stronger, drowning me.

Her body was hot as if her own little inferno was ignited by our contact and being the demon I was, I wanted more of it. I wanted to push her to beg for me even through her subconscious. I wanted to imprint myself into her mind so deep, all she could do was live and breathe me… the same way I did.

I hated her for it, nipping at the skin on her shoulder, then licking the pinkened flesh.

She gasped and scissored her legs, pulling my hand deeper into the core of her heat. I angrily obliged, slipping my hand into her panties to find them soaked with slick.

"I need you. Please." Her eyelids fluttered when I dipped a finger inside, scalding my fingertips with her feminine firestorm.

Her hips began to thrust rhythmically, rubbing her ass against my organ seeking a home and I growled against the nape of her neck. The smell of her perspiration made my throat water with the slaking need to taste her. Darting my tongue out, she exhaled when I licked across her shoulder from one side to the next.

But it wasn't enough. All it did was start a ravenous appetite that made me want to devour her whole. I warred with my natural instincts, reminding myself that as much as I wanted to consume her, I would be without an employee.

I would be without her annoying smiles and wicked playfulness as she caressed my phallus from outside my pants, showcasing a side of her that imprisoned me beneath her spell.

"Kimmy, you wretched little being. You dare ensnare a demon?" I whispered behind her ear, wanting to know her answer yet not wanting her to wake just yet.

"Yes," she whispered back and I pushed her shoulder down, coercing her onto her stomach with my weight while my tail pulled down the elastic waistband.

She shivered and moaned as my tail wrapped around her leg and pulled it apart. Running my nose down her lower back, I fought to hold back my form. But when her cloying arousal burned my nose, my flesh suit ripped to shreds around us.

With a snarl, I dove my tongue into her pussy and stretched her puffy skin. She tasted of the most forbidden hellfires as she drench my mouth with her slick.

"That's it. Be a good girl and come for your demon," I purred. She clenched herself around my tongue and I forced it deeper, wanting to pierce the depths of her innards until she was a part of me.

If this was the master's punishment, I was a glutton for it. Kimmy didn't disappoint as her little hands clawed into her sheets while she tried to squirm away from me. I grabbed her hips and pulled her back, making sure to get every last taste of her into my mouth before she cried out against her pillow in pleasure while I feasted on her sacrifice, impaling her pussy again and again with my tongue until her shaking stopped.

Running one last lick up her back side, I pulled her elastic waistband back up and groaned against her lower back as the moonlight made her tears gleam in the corner of her eye.

It was despicable of me to want to see her in tears. She shouldn't look as beautiful as she did when she was crying, so the fault lied solely in her hands. She drove me to this madness and now I was left with nothing but abominable longing until I saw her again.

Reluctantly removing myself from her side, I could feel the spikes along my skin pulsing with need as well as my cock. But I preferred to hear her consciously scream while I impaled her. Therefore, I would have to suffer a little longer.

"Dammit, Kimmy. You've bewitched me, you little fool," I grumbled before pulling her blanket over her resting form.

Who was I kidding? The only fool in the room was me.

Loathing myself, I left her apartment, making sure to secure the lock. The sound of a muffled cry caught my attention and I snapped my head to see the man across the hall re-enter his room once more. Why was this human operating against the saccadic rhythm typical for his kind?

There was something about him that was out of place. I stared at his closed door, rubbing my chin. The lingering taste of Kimmy, stole my attention and I cursed beneath my breath as I stomped down the stairs toward my Camaro.

I needed a ride to clear my mind. I couldn't go to work discombobulated like this. The little female would latch onto my weakness and I would be irrecoverable.

The last thing I needed were for the other demons to pity me for finding myself shackled to the one thing we lived to torture and devour.

CHAPTER 25

KIMMY

I lost track of how long I'd been working at The Good Char. They say time flies when you're having fun.

"Kimmy!" came his low tenor, the one that made me want to obey immediately. "Get into the back room."

"Yes, sir!" I squeaked, my heart palpitating.

Was it wrong of me to react in excitement and anticipation? I had been having weird dreams about my boss. It was so wrong of me. So naughty. I shouldn't be thinking of him this way, not when he commanded the very air around me while we were at work. But gosh, I wanted it to be true. These dreams were becoming more and more vivid. I found myself waking up soaked with sweat, too embarrassed to visit my parents until I washed myself twice after work.

I had visited them once, after I had a landline installed in my apartment. I bought some pastries and came over with the news that I was fully out on my own but I wasn't without means of reach.

My mother bawled while my father ranted about the bad influences of western culture. No matter how they tried to berate or guilt trip me, what was done was already done. I had my own place and everything was set up.

I slowly made my way to the back of The Good Char.

My boss... Dzik—these dreams would never allow me to look at him the same. I wanted to be more than friends. I bit my lip, knowing I had been giving him extra smiles and touching his arm when we talked. I was warring inside of myself because I knew he once mentioned that we needed to keep it strictly business. I had to respect that. Didn't I?

Though the lines had blurred more and more the longer we were around each other. And maybe I was wrong, but it didn't feel like it was solely me toeing on the other side of the forbidden.

Stop it, Kimmy. You're letting your attraction cloud your judgment. I sighed. I should be thinking about other things besides having my head up in the clouds.

They still hadn't found Cindy or the guys she was with. I had put up some missing person flyers around the area but no one had called my landline with any news yet.

Both Nicole and I hoped she would turn up

soon. I could use my best friend to talk about my feelings. It was different with Nicole. We didn't have that kind of relationship yet. And with us both silently grieving, it was hard to try to establish anything. The last time I saw her, she came by The Good Char to ask if I had heard anything. We both left a bit dejected that day.

I listened as Mr. Dzik turned off the neon sign and followed me into the backroom. He was always strange that way, preventing anyone from lining up when he wanted me to give him time. I secretly found it attractive, the way he did what he wanted, when he wanted. He was so bad, and it made me squirm with need. Sitting on the stack of flour, I thought back to the day he took care of me and flushed.

I liked the attention he gave, even if he was growling in my face. A mean man would have left me to tend to myself. Not Mr. Dzik. He swooped in without a word and made sure I was taken care of. Just thinking about it made me swoon again.

I saw through his exterior whether he realized it or not—and I continued to desire him more than an employee should.

I couldn't stop watching the way his stubbled jaw would flex when he was around me, or the way his shoulders would tense up when I caught him looking at me too.

Like now.

He cleared his throat and shoved an envelope

in front of me. "Your first couple of months went well," he said with absolutely no emotion.

A new excitement bubbled up within me. I was excited to see how much was in the envelope he was handing to me. Christmas was coming up and I had been feeling a little festive, but unsure of how much I could splurge on simple decorations for my apartment. I ripped it open and my eyes widened at the numbers. "Three hundred dollars? Holy crap!"

This was way more than the hours I worked. He was so kind to me. Oh, why did he keep making me fall more and more in love with him?

"Thank you Mr. Dzik!"

He groaned, the sound vibrating through my chest and down my body until I pressed my legs together, shooting my eyes toward his. I watched his nostrils flare, finally connecting it to when I found my body reacting to something simple he would do that made me more attracted to him.

Did he feel it too? Gosh, I really hoped he did.

"About the mister thing, let's just call me D or Dzik. Drop the mister, for the love of hell." His signature scowl quickly smoothed after a few moments. It was something else I noticed about him. He was different lately. Like right now, there seemed to be a mischievous glint in his eye. Was I missing something?

I smiled in response like I always did, but this time I could have sworn the crows feet at the corner of his eyes softened.

"If you keep working the way you do, I may actually be able to take a day off," he chuckled.

I beamed at him. That would be nice. I wanted to do that for him. He deserved it. He gave me a chance when he knew nothing about me. In fact, I don't even remember filling out any sort of application.

His voice cut through my thoughts. "Now get out of here, go have some fun." When he cracked a smile, my heart raced and I felt flustered. The world stopped and my eyes were glued to him. It was the first time I had seen it and it was glorious. No wonder he didn't smile much. How would we get any work done if girls started flocking The Good Char.

I didn't like the thought. Not one bit.

I gripped the check close to my chest and beamed at him again, letting him know how grateful I was.

He put a scowl back on his face as he pointed out the door.

I nodded, quickly took off my hat and apron and ran out the mall and got on my bike. This was more than my parents paid their cooks.

Hell yes! I'm a weiner dipper and I like it! Oh my god, I'm so freaking happy. He paid me so well. Now, what exactly was I going to do with this bonus money? I wanted to make sure that I made a difference and do some good with it.

I rode my bike up the street, my mind giddy, constantly thinking about what I could do with my money. Letting the breeze caress my skin under the Nevada sun, I snapped my head to the side when my eyes caught a glimpse of movement.

"What was that? Aww, it couldn't be!" I turned my head to see several stray kitties. And I loved kitties.

I knew exactly what I could do. I could take them to the vet and get their shots and then I could get them adopted out. This would be the perfect way to spend some of my money to give back and I owed it all to Mr. Dzik.

I pulled up to the nearby local grocery store and ran inside, looking for a worker.

"Hi! Excuse me! Can I have a large box please, if you have one available?"

The worker looked at me perplexed. "What do you need a box for?"

"Kittens!"

He gave me a crooked smile, shook his head and went to the back, returning with what I asked for.

"Thank you!"

He was very nice. *He was nice just like D. It felt weird calling Mr. Dzik anything else but maybe this was his way of us getting closer.* I still didn't understand why he thought pets were nonsense. Maybe if he had a cute little kitty, he wouldn't be so grumpy.

I grabbed the box from the worker and my mouth turned into a little 'o' of surprise. It was a super large box. It must have once been filled with watermelons or something because it was just the right size and smelled good.

"Can I leave my bike here for a few minutes while I take these little guys to the vet?" I asked him before he could go back to work.

The worker looked at me for a few moments. "Yeah, of course."

The mother cat was nowhere to be found when I returned. Oh no, she must have abandoned them. How could she do that?

"It's okay little guys. I'll take care of you. I hope your mother is alright." I looked around for a few more moments, hoping I could catch a glimpse of her hiding somewhere with no luck. "I promise I'll take care of your babies!" I called out before I happily gathered up the little fellas one at a time, listening to their little mewls and reassuring them I was going to take care of them.

I quickly made my way down the street and to the vet. I struggled a little to get myself and the box through the door but I managed it with help from someone who was leaving.

Blowing my frazzled hair out my face, the person at the counter addressed me. "Hello, young lady. May I help you with something?"

Tightly gripping onto the box, the kittens began to tumble and play. "Hi! Yes, I found these strays and I would like to get their shots so I can help get them adopted."

"Well, aren't you just the sweetest?" she smiled before leaning over the counter to peek into the box. She handed me some paperwork, then took the box from me. She informed me I could come by and pick them up tomorrow and gave me the cost.

"That's fine. My boss is an amazing man and I can afford it," I cheesed so hard. She didn't understand what I was talking about but that was okay. I knew in my heart what I was saying and I was proud to announce it to the world. I had the best boss on the planet.

It felt good to do something on my own, outside of buying necessities, without using money from my parents. I was also glad the kittens would get a chance to live a good life. I walked out of the vet's office smiling and twirling with my hands up to the sky.

When I finally made it home, I went straight to bed. I tossed and turned all night, wondering if they would ever find Cindy and if she was okay along with if the kittens would actually get adopted out. I eventually dozed off to dream of my boss wrapping my arm lovingly in bandage and leaning in toward my face.

CHAPTER 26

DZIK

It's been two days since my last visit here. Walking toward my apartment, I felt the air shift. When my breath came out in visible puffs, I swung around to find the master stand there.

Crap.

"Master..." I started, caving my shoulders in a little to bow.

"You wouldn't happen to know why there has been an influx of souls leaving this place, would you? I'm sure it is not a coincidence that I find you here," he said without emotion.

"If I said it was because of me, will it reduce my sentence?" I blurted out.

The master's eyes flamed and then darkened once more. "No."

I sighed dejectedly. "Then I won't claim it to be me, sadly."

He nodded his head and disappeared in a cloud of smoke before the atmosphere readjusted itself.

That was the first time he checked in on me. I wonder what was happening back in the underworld. Jealousy ripped through my throat and I frowned. They could all choke on their own tongues for all I care. Stomping toward the apartment building, I bypassed my lower level home and went directly up the next flight of stairs.

The sound of light metal scraping caught my ears just as I made it up the final step... to find the male from across the hall trying to mess with Kimmy's locks.

"What the hell are you doing?" I barked out.

Failing to hide behind his hoodie, he dropped his tools and ran. But I was faster. I let him unlock his door and swing it open, then tackled him to the ground and dug my demon claws into the side of his neck to keep him subdued.

He cried like every other pathetic human. Hopefully he wouldn't piss like the last one.

I leaned in and licked up some of the blood that began to bead from his pierced flesh.

"What are you hiding here, human? The smell of stale blood is strong in this room."

"G-Get off me!"

"Or else what?" I growled. "You going to kill me like you did the last woman you had here? I can still smell her piss and shit. In fact, I'm confident you're the reason why the master paid me a visit."

"W-What the hell are you?" He coughed out

and I dug my fingers deeper, feeling around his tendons. An idea struck me like the master's whip and a menacing smile grew.

"I'm your first nightmare, the rest will find you in the afterlife. Send the other demons my regards," I cackled before I snatched a few of his tendons out while ripping the corner of his mouth. He was gurgling on his own blood and bile before he could get a scream out.

The dark liquid began to pool around us, seeping into the woodwork of the floor in intricate linear patterns as I continued to dismember him. Melkgard would lecture my ear off about ruining the meat, but it wasn't about that this time.

No, he was going to satisfy a different kind of craving boiling inside of me.

I listened to his gurgled cries as I continued to claw into his flesh, stripping it one at a time, watching the way it peeled like melted stringed cheese from his muscles. The more tendons I exposed, the more I gleefully laughed as I saved them to the side, separating muscle from bone.

My hands began to slip as I slowly became bored with the fact that he stopped screaming. He couldn't even stay alive for my entertainment, the insolent human.

Gathering my prizes, I walked out of his apartment as the sound of chitter chatters appeared behind me. I slowly made my way to Kimmy's door, memorizing the new scratches on her knob before pulling out my key.

I took off my boots and dropped my prizes the moment I made it inside and made my way soundlessly to her bedside. She was a deep sleeper, her light snores a catalyst to my dark desires.

Lifting her shirt, I drew on her pebbled skin with the blood coating my fingers. Continuing to trail them with intentional patterns, I stared at my demon name before leaning down to clean the blood off her.

Repeating the motion with blood and tongue, I traveled down her navel to the strong scent of her desire. Chitter chatters came in waves as the sprites curiously watched what I was doing.

Their voyeuristic tendencies made my possessive nature amplify. Growling against the apex of her legs, she gasped in her sleep as I once again forced her to give me what I craved while she remained unconscious and blissfully unaware of the monster between her legs.

With the scent of blood, the adrenaline of the fresh kill still in my veins, my pleasure was amplified beyond measure as she squirmed around in her bed innocently while trying to break my neck with her closing thighs.

My horns sprouted atop my head, slowly inching its way into a curl as my flesh suit tore further and further along my skull. Only Kimmy could bring me such pain and contentment at the same damn time.

"Mr. Dzik, please," she moaned, her brows furrowing while her eyes remained closed.

I pierced her pussy with a few of my fingers alongside my thumb, stretching her beyond her little body's capabilities. Thoughts of burying my phallus deep in her womb made me want to combust. I groaned, on my knees worshiping her as she shook and gave me what I craved.

"That's a good girl," I whispered against her skin, retracting my tongue then making sure to clean any evidence of blood left behind. Her scent was intoxicating and I may or may not have intentionally left a light wound on her inner thigh as evidence of my midnight claim.

When I removed myself, I scowled at the bloodstains on her sheets, but there was nothing to be done about it now.

Running a hand down my face, I forced myself to once again, leave her side and torture myself until she returns to work the next day.

Shoving my feet into my boots, I realized they wouldn't fit because they had elongated into something inhuman.

"Blasted hell," I grumbled, licking my lips to calm myself with her taste. Grabbing my things, I opened her door and took one last look at her beneath the moonlight's glow.

With her dark hair splayed behind her, I began to wonder if she was sent here from the enemy... and if a demon could ever tame an angel.

My thoughts morose, I descended the steps and made my way to my own humble abode.

Throwing my boots aside, I went down my latch and sat myself on the only furniture inside.

A few sprites popped in and I waited begrudgingly to see if I would receive more visitors. Luckily for me, none came.

"I need to stop the madness. What was she doing to me?" I said to no one in particular.

Disgusted with myself, my agitation grew when one of the sprites popped beside me, trying to take a seat on my atrocious couch. I grabbed its neck until its eyes exploded then grinned. It writhed in my grasp, trying to claw its own face as I pulled out its fangs until the writhing waned.

Breaking his neck, I pulled his head and spine out of its body then began to dig into his flesh to collect the bones to add to my little collection.

CHAPTER 27

KIMMY

As I was awakened by the sound of birds singing outside my window, a smile crept on my face.

It was time to go to work.

Eww. Why was I so sticky? Maybe I was having night sweats. I blushed. With all these sensual dreams I had been having about a certain man, it wouldn't be a surprise. I made sure to shower twice.

When I came back out, I realized there was blood on my sheets. Did I start my period early? I giggled behind my hand. If only my mother could see me now. She wouldn't be able to ask if I was pregnant because the evidence was right there. I needed to get another set of sheets though. Rolling my eyes, I continued to get ready for work.

Saturday was one of the busiest days of the week for us. I got myself ready, glad I turned on the water to my apartment, and walked outside only to remember that I left my bike at the grocery store. I had gone back to get it when I went to check up on the kittens and then got distracted at the store again, talking to the employee that helped me get a box.

I didn't think I had time to detour to get my bike. I was going to have to foot it to work today. It was only a couple of miles.

It was warm like any other day and when I finally made it to work, I was sweating. The walk was further than I remembered but I couldn't wait to tell my boss what he had helped me do. I was so excited that I could barely get the words out of my mouth when I saw him wiping down the counters.

He actually waved at me with his rag when he saw me come in. It made my already elated heart jump for joy. He was happy today.

"Did you enjoy your evening?" he asked while he stirred the batter.

"I bet you can't guess what I did with my last check!" I singsonged in his direction.

"I don't really care. It was your money. I'm happy you enjoy working here, but we can keep our personal life separate." He moved from the batter to adding more wieners to the grill.

"I know Mr. Dzik, but I have to tell you. If it wasn't for you, I wouldn't have been able to take care of those little kittens I found and now they have a bright future instead of dying on the streets. The vet tech even asked me if I wanted one for myself. It's all because of you. Thank you so much!"

I just wanted to hug him in gratitude, but I wasn't sure where we stood since the incident that shall not be named. He was such an amazing guy and I couldn't help but admire him more and more as he continued to do his duties. A man shouldn't look that attractive with an apron on, but here he was, making me lust after him with every stretch and flex of his tanned arm.

I quickly grabbed some paper towels to wipe my brow and readjust my ponytail before grabbing my hat and placing it on my head. I couldn't wait to see how the kittens were doing at the end of the shift today. The vet tech said she had already received some interest.

I hummed a little tune and danced to the beat in my head as I leaned over the counter and began to wave at the potential customers in the area with a bright smile.

A couple of teenage boys laughing together caught sight of me and smiled, waving in my direction. I didn't know who they were but they seemed friendly so I waved back, hoping they'd come by the counter.

They took two steps forward and their smiles fell before they quickly turned and walked away. I wonder what that was about. Maybe one of them needed to use the restroom or something.

I straightened and my back hit something solid. I yelped and turned to find Mr. Dzik standing behind me, staring after the boys. Did I miss something?

"You shouldn't lean over the counter like that," he told me bluntly.

"Why? Is it dirty? Sorry, I should have cleaned it first."

He cleared his throat and looked over at the grill. "Button up your shirt, Kimmy."

"What?" I quickly looked down and forgot that I had unbuttoned it on the way because I was getting so sweaty on the walk here. I quickly redid them and grabbed one of the flyers on the counter and began to fan myself. The mall air conditioning felt amazing but my body had yet to fully cool down.

"Why is your face flush after those humans waved at you? Do you know them? Don't bring your friends around here, you got it? This is a place of work and I will not have you dilly dallying around during work hours."

I was so confused.

"N-No. I don't know them. I was just waving hoping they'd come over to buy some wieners."

Mr. Dzik did something I could never antici-pate. He grabbed me by the arm and pulled me to the back room, shutting the door dramatically. *Oh no.* Was I in trouble for something? I shouldn't have ever talked back. Didn't my parents always teach me not to talk back? I was going to get fired, wasn't I?

Mr. Dzik backed me up against the wall and

leaned down, snarling in my face. "You shouldn't hope for any male to come in your direction, do you understand?"

Huh?

"You don't want customers to come to The Good Char?"

The air around us changed and suddenly it felt heavier than when I was walking under the sun.

"I don't care about any blasted customers when they're looking at you like meat on a stick. If they value their lives, they'll keep their distance."

I blinked a few times, trying to understand what was going on when his face began to waver and I wondered if I was overheated from the walk.

"Mr....Dzik, I-I..." why was my brain feeling foggy?

He must have known I wasn't feeling well, maybe that was why he pulled me back here. How very kind of him. In fact, with his proximity and my eyes glued to his lips and the way they moved, I think I did need to sit down for a moment. Was he talking to me?

"I-I think I need to sit down—" Before I could finish my sentence, my head became light and I fell forward.

CHAPTER 28

DZIK

THERE WAS SOMETHING TERRIBLY WRONG WITH ME today. I was anxious for her arrival. I watched the clock as the hand slowly crept to the next minute wondering where the hell she was. She was never this late. She was always here at least ten minutes before the official opening and it was already nine minutes til.

My skin prickled and my back tensed the moment I sensed her presence. It was the smile and look of pure joy on her face that made her practically glow as she made her way to the counter, singing a happy upbeat song.

Must she always come in so...loudly? I found that though she still annoyed me, she no longer agitated me.

She placed her hand over her mouth endearingly as she giggled, relaying to me her tales of saving tiny beasts from dying on the streets.

"Now they have a bright future. It's all because of you. Thank you so much!"

Now, wait a blasted minute. Was she accusing me of assisting her in her good deed? This female is going to be the death of me. I was gonna end up banished in the human realm forever.

As I pondered what to do to counteract what happened, the hairs on the back of my neck rose as I watched her wave at a couple of young human males across the mall. Possessiveness took over me and all I saw was red from their limbs being torn apart. The last kill didn't nearly satisfy my lust for it as much as I thought it would.

Didn't she realize that the claim was already made? She made it, for demon's sake! How dare she tempt others when I was standing right beside her. I walked up behind and glared in their direction, threatening to peel their eyelids off mentally. My skin itched to take off their heads and shove them into Justin's dough. They must have felt the death aura I was sending in their direction because they quickly left the vicinity without me having to cross the other side of the counter. *Good.*

I needed to make things clear to her simple little mind. Perhaps she just needed a reminder. I pulled her to the back room to give her a piece of my mind. She responded by widening her large, dark innocent eyes but I wouldn't fall for her tricks. Not this time. No, this time, she would understand exactly who the master was around The Good Char.

But she had another trick up her sleeve I didn't anticipate. Her eyes fluttered as she fell forward and I quickly caught her before she could hit the ground. Of course, her plan to deter my anger would work. My anger quickly morphed into trepidation as I dragged her over to one of the folding chairs and lifted her onto my lap.

I gnashed my teeth at the situation, confused as to how we got here. But the longer I stared at her unconscious form, the more I was lost in her presence surrounding me.

"One shouldn't look this enticing while unconscious, Kimmy. Your womanly wiles never fail to tempt me," I grumbled.

Of course, she didn't answer. I gently wiped her brow and pushed back some of her strands as her striped hat fell to the ground softly. Her skin was hot. I didn't think humans ran this high in temperature but what did I know? Most of them were being burned alive back home.

Gently tapping her face, I called out her name to no avail. I could feel my flesh suit ready to tear apart as my vehemence over this uncontrollable situation coursed through me.

With a split decision, I got to my feet with her cradled in my arms and gently laid her down on the bags of dried batter ingredients. Making sure she wouldn't fall off the mound, I took off my apron and swiftly made my way to the main area of Hellscape Mall.

I needed Pashar's advice and aid. I couldn't go back to the underworld with this. The other demons wouldn't let me live it down if they found out. As luck would have it, Pashar's shop, Dark Spell Comics, was on the first floor.

I made my way through his doors and he snapped his head up from where he stood behind his dark counter.

"What the bloody hell do you want?" he greeted me.

"I need your assistance. How does one revive an unconscious human?"

He tilted his head curiously without leaving his spot.

"And why would you want to do that? Are you having a problem killing humans now, Dzik? Has the human realm softened you? Are you developing some sort of dysfunction?"

I stomped toward his counter and brought our faces nose to nose. He didn't back down from the challenge. His eyes bored into mine with the same hatred I had for him.

"I need to revive my human, Pashar. She seemed to have overheated herself on her way to work. At least, that's my assumption. I also need..." I casted my gaze at his store and wares. "A book on how to coerce a human to stay with a demon."

Pashar threw his head back and cackled and my hands turned to fists on top of his counter.

"Look here, you bloody stupid demon. There are no books on how to coerce a human to stay with you. You just make them! Did you lose your demon card while you were here?" He shook his head in utter disappointment and I snarled, biting the air in front of me.

He ignored it and leaned into my face.

"I suggest you get your ass out of my store, demon. There's nothing that will help you here."

"Fine!" I barked out. "I need to get some fleas, can you at least do that?"

His eyes sparkled as an evil grin broke across his face.

"Why, I may indeed be able to help you with that..."

I left the store in a sour mood. At least I was able to obtain some fleas. I was going to find Kimmy's little rescued beasts and infect them. I was not going to be accused of being an accomplice to any good deed while I was serving my time here. The master was going to see just how evil I could be and what havoc I could wreak.

Good luck adopting these stupid kittens out if they have fleas, I snickered to myself. No, that little female wouldn't get me anymore years stuck here in this wretched fairytale land.

When I made it back, Kimmy was still unconscious on the mounds of batter. I put my hands on my hips, wondering what the hell my next move would be. How did one wake up an unconscious human? This was exactly why there needed to be a handbook on these matters.

An idea formed in my head and I made my way to the sink, gathering a pitcher of water. *This should do the trick.* Killing two birds with one stone and all. I did like killing and it was a demony thing to do. I nodded my head as I made my way to the back room and splashed her face with water. She sputtered and quickly came to. I puffed out my chest in triumph until I realized I could see her breasts clearly from here.

Thoughts of those boys coming back around to specifically see her in this state grated my nerves. With a growl, I lifted her up with the intent on finding her another set of uniform to wear. But I got sidetracked when her arms wrapped around me as she continued to gasp for air, pushing her round mounds against my chest. Something inside of me rumbled and I found myself nuzzling the crook of her neck, taking in her scent that has haunted my every waking hour.

Did she always have to smell this good?

"What happened, D?" she whispered against me.

My tail mentally swished at her little nickname she whispered in her sleep. Her voice seeped into my demon skin as if in a caress and I could no longer help myself. I licked the water trailing down her exposed skin and she sharply inhaled.

It was different when she was awake. Her little reactions made my ego inflate.

When her little hands began to massage my neck and head, I was lost. Our lips found one another and we frantically began to devour each other's faces as if in a race against time.

I didn't forget my mission and broke the kiss in order to quickly divest her of her wet clothes. Her eyes widened as her hands quickly moved to unfasten my pants and I choked, warring against myself if I should stop her or not.

Bloody hell. When her hand gripped my phallus with a strength I didn't know she had, The Good Char's master turned into a servant and we both fell back onto the bags of batter, exploding one of them into a cloud of dust all around us.

We both coughed and waved our hands in front of our faces, but quickly closed the distance between ourselves as our mouths continued to explore each other's bodies.

"I need you, D," she admitted with a tone laced with the same lust I felt for nights. "I can't stop thinking about you."

I growled at her command and quickly kicked off my boots, then removed my pants, freeing the beast between my legs once and for all. It wept against her skin as I divested her of her coverings, forcing her legs around my hips.

She cradled my face and our frenzied kiss slowed. I didn't understand why there was a shift and was desperate to get back to where we once were. Nipping her jaw, I trailed kisses down to the top of her breasts, wishing I could be in my demon form to take a bite out of her and see what she truly tasted like. This human tongue was lacking in comparison to what I could truly experience.

Since I couldn't, I had to do the next best thing. She squealed when I folded her in half and made my way between her legs with my face. I slapped my hand over her mouth to muffle her cries before the other vendors could hear us. If we were back home in the underworld, I would make it my mission to make her scream for the other demons to hear, but alas, we are stuck in the human realm for now.

"Open up for me, like a good little human. I need to taste you. I deserve it after what you put me through," I growled. I wasn't about to ask her for something I had already been taking at my leisure. But she didn't need to know that.

She's been nothing but a menace since she barged into my life. She deserved to be punished for it—awake or not.

She said something against my hand but I didn't care to hear it as I dove my tongue inside of her and groaned against her taste. This was probably what human addicts went through. I didn't feel sorry for them one bit. They did it to themselves the same way I did it to myself, night in and night out. When her blunt teeth threatened to pierce the skin of my fingers, I pressed my mouth harder against her. She was trying to rile me up, make me lose control. But I would show her. I would show her that this demon was the most evil she had ever encountered.

Kimmy reacted beautifully to every pass of my tongue. When I pushed a finger inside of her, she wrapped her legs around my head and threatened to break it with her thighs. I took every challenge she threw my way. Nipping and torturing her pussy, paying extra attention to the mark I left behind the other night.

She mewled against my hand and I trembled beneath my ministrations. Every time her body wound up and her thighs threatened to squeeze my head to oblivion, I slowed my torture. She began to cry against my palm and I gave her a wicked smile, watching her face as she watched mine with unbridled lust.

"If you scream, Kimmy. I will kill you." Her eyes rolled back in carnal desire and my demon skin expanded in pride. "I want to devour you. But not like the others, no. I want to savor every inch of you alive and feel your veins throb against my skin."

When I slipped my tongue into her again and flicked it upward, her body shook and she slapped her own hands over her mouth to stifle the scream that threatened to rent the air.

My body heaved as I lapped up everything she offered me in sacrifice and suddenly, an unexpected sound rented the air and I felt my physical tail whipping back and forth.

CHAPTER 29

KIMMY

Did he just—

Did he just pass gas?

He crawled up my body and I patted him on his back. "It's okay. It happens to the best of us. It's only natural."

I tried my best to comfort him. After all, I didn't want his embarrassment to derail our little tryst. To be honest, I was the one that was embarrassed. The furthest I went with anyone was a fumbling third base with Jim when we were juniors in high school. That and listening to all of Cindy's wild, detailed tales.

"What?" he mumbled, licking my stomach and giving me goosebumps.

I lifted my head up to comfort him again when my entire body froze at the sight in front of me. "M-Mr. Dzik."

He nipped my skin and crawled up to lick my shoulder. "It's Dzik. Say it with me, Kimmy. Dzik."

I tentatively cradled his face and reached up to touch the quadruple horns that now protruded out of his head in a curve, intertwining in different directions. "Dzik...you have horns."

He snapped his head up and something whipped my outer thigh. I squealed and he covered my mouth again with his hand before he looked over himself and cursed under his breath. When he pulled his hand away from my mouth and turned it over, some of his knuckles were busted and spikes protruded out the back of his hand, revealing skin a very familiar color to our wieners.

"What's happening, Dzik? Are you okay? Do I need to call the police? Do I need to call area fifty one?" My concern quickly rocket launched beyond anxiety. I was flat freaking out.

He growled before slamming his mouth on mine and a very different tongue entered into me. I was already hot and bothered and the touch of fear growing within me took my arousal to new heights. I knew I was a freak on the inside with my love for movies like The Black Lagoon. Whoever said they weren't attracted to that monster was a liar. Cindy used to tell me how she would diddle herself to thoughts of him back in high school. That only led me down a road to do the same.

"Dzik, I—" I didn't know what else to say. When was opening time anyway?

His long tongue dove down my throat and I

gagged. He groaned as if he could barely contain himself as he pulled his tongue back to wrap around mine seductively. My breast felt heavy and tender against his body the more he rubbed himself against me. He was such a large man to begin with but whatever was happening right now made him feel so much larger.

"Your mouth has caused me nothing but grief, Kimmy. And now it tortures me. Do you like how you taste?" he panted against my lips. "I could tie you to this mound and feast on you until you beg me to take your soul."

Sweet lord, who was this man? *Was he even a man at all?*

As if he read my mind, he grinded his dick against me and I gasped in surprise. This was not the same as I felt earlier. It left a trail of wetness on my inner thigh as ridges and something else that was moving. Or maybe it was me who was squirming?

"Do you have protection?" I panted against his mouth. Dzik refused to let me up for air as he continued to give me drugging kisses. All my senses were overtaken by everything that was him. I couldn't think straight.

He pulled away from me and his eyes glowed an eerie mix of yellows and browns and I was mesmerized. Did I think he was handsome before?

"I left my battle axe back home," he replied. I scrunched my face and he chuckled deliciously against my cheek. I blushed in response. "But I brought another beast in its stead."

I was going to end up pregnant. My mother was right. It didn't matter that I was creeping toward my mid twenties. The man was too virile. I couldn't convince myself to push him off me. Not when his hands were worshiping my body with his caresses along my sides and breasts. Both guilt and shame coursed through me as well as a thrill of the forbidden, especially because he was so much older *and* my boss.

What would it feel like with him buried deep inside of me?

When his tongue stretched out to lave at my nipple and pull it, I moaned and wrapped my arms around him tighter. If Cindy were here, she'd tell me you only live once. And she was right.

"Open your legs for me, Kimmy, before I tear you in two. You're going to take me either way."

What if I wanted him to? It sounded appealing. My old ex Jim had only rubbed his dick against me skin to skin. It couldn't be that much different, right?

"I'm so horny for you right now," I told him. It was the truth. I didn't know if it was unsexy to say, but there it was.

"Then open wider for me, my little flesh morsel. I'm going to make sure every male around you knows exactly who you belong to."

Oh sweet heaven above.

When the large, bulbous head of his cock

pressed against the apex of my legs, I tried my best to relax myself but when the skin of his shoulder began to stretch apart like string cheese, I got distracted and tightened up.

He groaned against my shoulder, licking it and grazing it with teeth that were much too sharp to be human.

"D. I-I'm nervous. I've never—"

"—copulated with a demon before. Good. And no other demon will touch you but me." He ended his sentence with a thrust and I could feel my pussy stretch deliciously around him to the brim.

"I can't. You're too—" I was blabbering at this point. It was uncomfortable but I didn't want him to stop. My hands clawed at his back and I swore it felt like my nails were coming away with more of his flesh as ridged skin and spikes broke through his skin.

"You will, little carrion." He thrusted again and my body was forced to accommodate his size. Did he just say he cared for me? I didn't have time to think about when I was distracted by his tongue laving my jaw right before he grabbed my chin and forced my face toward his for another kiss. It was drugging and I was under his spell, very much a willing participant to see where we were going from here.

He surged his hips forward and swallowed my cries as he buried himself to the hilt, making me feel like he was going to come out of my throat. My stomach was distended and I could feel something pushing against it. I screeched but he stuck his very inhuman finger into my mouth and distracted me once again from what he was doing.

And whatever it was, made me feel so good. I was euphoric as he continued to thrust into me at a harsh pace. When he pulled his finger out and pushed the back of my thighs up, I thought I would pass out from his invasion. I couldn't anticipate my body convulsing from the orgasm that hit me like a ton of bricks. I jerked so hard, we both fell onto the floor in a pile of limbs, but he didn't stop. Dzik simply turned me onto my stomach and lifted my butt into the air as he inserted himself and continued to pound into my tender flesh.

Hands reached over and grabbed my breasts. Hands slid down my sides and grabbed my hips. I was suddenly so overstimulated, I lost count of what was touching me. Pleasure began to climb in tune to his rapid pace when his fingers crept to the apex of my legs and began to play with my clit. I couldn't fight the ecstasy, the top half of my body fell forward and my hands clawed at the tiled floor as a splash gushed between us with him still inside.

Oh god. Did he come? Did I pee myself? What just happened.

Dizk groaned and agonizingly slowed his thrusts, as my body went through waves and waves of an orgasm that wanted to kill me. Tears flooded the floor as I mewled and arched my back, wanting to pull away and craving more all at once.

Dzik leaned over and covered my body, trailing kisses along my shoulder blade. "My little carrion is a squirter. It burns me that you wanted to mark me the same way I'm going to mark you."

Is that what it was? Embarrassment consumed me as he quickly pulled out, making me squirt again before invading me with another thrust.

"I'm going to breed you, my little carrion. I'm going to fill you with my spawn," he panted.

Before I could cry out for him to stop torturing me, he increased his pace, sliding me across the floor until he groaned and snarled, biting down on my shoulder as my body was thrown into another orgasm I didn't think I could take.

My body limply fell to its side as I tried to catch my breath, darkness threatening my vision.

Voices came from the other side of the wall but it all sounded like a low buzz as Dzik pulled my body against his and began to nuzzle the back of my head, occasionally licking the wound on my shoulder that was throbbing.

"Hey! Are you open today? I want a corndog!" was the last thing I heard as my tired body gave into the encroaching void of slumber.

CHAPTER 30

DZIK

She was beautiful when she was unconscious. And beautiful when she was taking my cock.

I cleaned her up the best I could while waiting for the wayward customers to leave. Intruders were more like it. Didn't they know that important matters needed to be completed back here.

Possessiveness crawled along my flesh like maggots the longer I stared at her relaxed form. I couldn't leave her here. I didn't trust any of the other humans to not take advantage of my little carrion.

Bending down, I grabbed one of my extra shirts and covered her in it before lifting her in my arms. Backing into the door, I quickly looked left and right to make sure no one else was around. It was times like this I was glad for the construction beside us.

Quickly making my way to the front counter, I threw the 'we're closed' sign on top and jumped into the vortex grill with my female safely tucked in my arms.

"Dzik. You're not due to be back for another day. Are the humans consuming that quickly?" came Zychor's voice.

I growled at him and shoved his shoulder aside with my own as I made my way to my original chambers back home in the mountainside.

Gently laying Kimmy down on my bed, I called for my old sprite companion, Fenia. The sprite quickly poofed into the room, flapping her necrotic wings rapidly.

"Have you returned home, Dzik? Is your sentence finally over?"

I scowled at the reminder. "I need you to take care of her until I can repair my flesh suit. Do not let her leave this chamber and do not answer too many of her questions if she wakes."

Fenia's head was practically attached to her shoulders sans a neck as she flew around the new specimen on my bed curiously. Straggly hair wisped around her as her wings beat faster and faster akin to the hummingbirds seen in the human realm.

Not waiting for her answer, I quickly left to find the demon who helped me pick out this flesh suit the first time.

A few questions and curses later, I was back to my intact human form and stomped my way toward my chambers to find Kimmy sitting in the middle of the bed, with her back to me.

I approached her cautiously, unsure of what she would make of her new surroundings when she squeaked and looked over her shoulder at me. The moment her eyes met mine, they shone with welcome as she scrambled off the bed and threw her arms around me.

"You're back! I thought you had left me. I woke up and wondered if I landed in some weird beach resort but then I realized that this looked more like a cave than a hotel. I mean, a beach trip would be nice for a date, you know? That's what I thought was happening. But did we even close the shop? What if customers are lined up waiting for us?"

The only way to stop her incessant chattering was to kiss her. She immediately molded against me and I could feel my tail threaten to rip through again to wrap itself around her.

I ended the kiss with a nip on her lip and cleared my throat. "How long have you been awake? Were you taken care of?"

"Oh yes. Your little flying friend—a sprite she called herself, I think—was very nice. She reminded me of you."

I grumbled. "I am not a nice person, Kimmy. I'm a demon."

She gave me a beaming smile and got on her tippy toes to plant a chaste kiss on my lips deflating my puffed chest. "Oh, I know. I mean, it took me a while to figure it out, but I did."

I narrowed my eyes in suspicion at her reaction. "Are you not scared, my little carrion? Do you not know where you are?"

I spread my arms with emphasis to our surroundings. The cries of human torture, wavering in the background as the volcanic eruptions threatened to steal the show.

She stood there, smiling.

This little female was proving to be more than meets the eye—if my true form had eyes.

"I know that you care about me, and sent someone to make sure I was alright when I woke up," she nodded, completely oblivious to her surroundings. This was exactly why she needed a demon like me to claim her. She wouldn't survive very long without one by her side.

"We need to get back. Come, Kimmy. The Good Char awaits its mistress."

She let out a raw laugh and my tail did rip out again which only made her laugh harder as it wrapped around her leg and caressed her hip. When she cradled my face and kissed me, I felt my entire body expand and all that was left was my true form.

She pulled back and her eyes widened with a mixture of both fear and lust. My phallus throbbed in reaction and I groaned in frustration and annoyance. She would be the death of me at this point. The master would never forgive me for bringing her here if I got caught.

Her fingers began to explore my face, one that was striated and torn, melted away and reformed until all that was left was exposed teeth and holes where my human nose should be. My horns itched with its freedom and as if she felt it, her little fingers grazed across where skin met bone, making me shiver.

"I'm going to need you to stay out of trouble," I exhaled. "I shall return." Needing to repair my flesh suit, yet again, I left her.

She nodded with a dazed smile and ten minutes later upon my return she continued to stand there, patiently waiting for me with her hands clasped in front of her like the first time she forced herself into my life. Fenia must have found the black dress she was wearing that showcased her curves more than it should. I would have to punish her for that later.

Grabbing her hand, I quickly made my way back to Zychor and his portal. She squealed as I grabbed the back of her knees and lifted her into my arms. Maybe I just wanted to feel her arms wrap around me, needing me. I could hear Belchar's voice asking me questions about who the human in my arms was and a new emotion reared its ugly head. I bared my teeth at him right before we leaped through and landed on the other side of The Good Char.

Luckily, no one was around. I pulled us both to the backroom and grabbed her hat, gently placing it on her head.

"You really are the perfect man, Dzik," she sighed happily.

I scowled and put on my own apron. "I'm not a man, Kimmy. Don't let this flesh suit fool you. What you see is simply what was required to blend in with the humans. The only reason I'm here is because of a sentence I must serve."

She gasped and I turned to look at her.

Her eyes shone with surprise and morbid curiosity. "Ooo! I knew you were a bad boy, D!"

I rolled my eyes, a bad habit I picked up from the little female before me and grumbled as I pulled her out to the front and took away the 'we're closed' sign.

Without missing a beat, Kimmy leaned across the counter, smiled and waved at the closest victims pulling customers in with her disgustingly happy aura.

Watching her cheerily perform her menial job and the smiles she brought to everyone around her, I had to admit...brought a smirk of pride to my face as well.

When we finished the last of the customers before closing, she looked over to me and winked, blowing a kiss which I pretended to catch and throw into the deep fry oil with pseudo revulsion.

Her laugh tinkled like a sweet melody and made everyone's eyes turn our way, prickling my possession into overdrive.

CHAPTER 31

KIMMY

We went a few more weeks stealing kisses and making love in awkward locations during the slow hours at The Good Char.

One random day, D showed up at my doorstep in all black and a leather jacket. He was a sight to behold—every woman's fantasy came to life.

"What are you doing here? Not that it's not a nice surprise. Do you want to come inside?" I was hoping he said yes when he gave me a crooked smirk, making my heart palpitate.

"I always come inside, little carrion. Make no mistake," he replied confidently, taking a step inside.

I sputtered and closed the door, trying to fan myself from his crude words. He was so naughty and I loved him that way.

I bit my bottom lip. As many times as I had

told him I loved him in my daydreams, I don't think I ever had the confidence to tell him out loud.

I know he desires my body, his actions proved it time and time again. But love? Could a demon love a human?

Before I could take a step, D caged me in against the door and my eyes widened.

"Have you been causing trouble?" He purred. It was something he asked frequently beneath his breath when we stole moments together. I think he loved punishing me for what he deemed as transgressions.

I giggled and his nostrils flared before he leaned in and took a deep inhale.

My giggles turned into gasps when my little kitten, Molly, began to growl at scratch at his boots. For some reason she comically despised D.

"Why haven't you gotten rid of this creature yet?" D barked out and I laughed.

I cradled his face and gave him a chaste kiss on the nose, ignoring his scowl. "Because she reminds me of you," I told him lovingly.

"Impossible. I am nothing like that little wretched, freeloading fur ball."

"You're so silly. You know, the other day the poor little thing was covered in fleas. I don't know how it happened but I had some extra funding left over from my last check so I was able to buy her the best shampoo. It made her black fur glisten so nicely. I'm so happy the others got adopted out.

But I'm grateful they kept one just for me," I gushed.

"The little furry Cretin," he grumbled under my breath and I giggled, grabbing his hand and pulling him to my newly covered loveseat.

"Do you like the couch cover? I was finally brave enough to invite my mother over the other day since it's more presentable now. I was so nervous she would complain and berate me about my choices. But after a few bouts of ugly cries, she left here with the understanding that I was committed on my path," I smiled sadly and D cupped my face.

I omitted the fact that she was still trying to push Mrs. Chen's son onto me, stating he just opened up his own firm with multiple people working under him. I finally told her that I was interested in someone else but refused to name who. As for my father, he still hasn't agreed to come visit but I was going to worry about that another day. One little victory at a time.

1986 came faster than I anticipated and I was much more content in life. Oh! And we found Cindy.

She ended up somewhere I never thought she would be.

D refuses to tell me the details but it involved a deal with another demon who was very reluctant to let her go. After I let her settle and her parents rejoiced in their reunion, I called her up one day to ask her about it.

"*Are you really alright, Cin?*" *I asked again, twirling the cord around my finger, waiting for her answer.*

"*More than alright. I'm glad I don't have to stare at that asshole Melkgard anymore. He annoyed me beyond belief day in and day out.*" *Her tone kept rising and I could hear her breathing heavier and heavier into the receiver.*

"*I'm just glad you're back. And hey, I'm sorry about the fight we had before you... you know. I missed you terribly and tried everything I could to find you.*" *I laughed humorlessly.* "*I bet some of the missing person posters are still up around your house.*"

"*I saw that,*" *her voice softened.* "*I'm sorry too, Kimmy. Gosh, if I could go back in time...*"

I was pulled from my memory by a familiar gruff voice.

"Your attention needs to be on me, little carrion. Nothing else," D hummed, leaning in to plant soft kisses on my throat.

"You're always on my mind, D. How could you not be? You take over my senses every time you're in a room with me," I admitted with a blush.

"The way your skin flushes makes mine want to break free."

I blushed further, thinking of all the last time he took me in his true form. "I'd like that," I whispered, intentionally enticing him.

He growled and nipped my skin before pulling back. His eyes danced with different colors again and I pressed my legs together. "A new bed will be delivered tomorrow. I'm not having the toddler sized bed you have now in my home."

I blinked a few times, trying to understand what he was saying. Did he—Did he just move in with me?

A smile bloomed on my face and he grinned in response, a peek of his fang showing through.

Before I could force him into a compromising position, he quickly pulled out something from his pocket and shoved it into my cleavage.

"What's this?" I asked curiously, turning the little box in my hands.

"Open it."

I squealed in delight as I pulled away the little blood red ribbon and revealed what was inside.

My jaw dropped at the pieces before me. An intricate necklace made from various materials shone under my light. Was that a jaw bone from something? I brought it up closer and examined the chain. It was made from a white material I didn't recognize, tightly braided together in a sturdy fashion. It was the matching earrings that stole the show. Intricately carved on an ivory colored material, I was almost afraid to wear it anywhere.

My eyes blurred and I sniffed.

"What the hell is wrong now? I thought human females liked gifts," he growled, rubbing the back of his neck. "I didn't know when your birthday was, so I figured I'd start the new year with this," he grumbled dejectedly.

I carefully closed the box, and then threw my arms around him, knocking him on his back. Peppering his face with kisses, I squealed again whispering how much his gift meant to me.

Somewhere between my kisses and my gratitude, my tongue slipped. "I love you, D."

His hands gripped my hips harder, making me squirm. "I would kill for you again and again even if you didn't love me, little carrion. Because you're mine. Don't even think about leaving me."

I threw my head back and laughed as he lifted me up bridal style and carried me to bed while the sun began to set.

The night brought on a different kind of dream this time. Lost in a haze of lust and sweat, I writhed in the sheets, trying to find reprieve. There was a soft hum against my skin and my hands crawled down to the back of someone's hand. It swatted me away and I blinked a few times, lost in limbo. Was I still dreaming? Was I waking up?

I took a sharp inhale when something hard and large impaled my pussy from behind.

"Be a good girl and go back to sleep," came a gruff, familiar masculine voice.

Was I ever going to stop having these naughty dreams about my demon? Maybe that was one of his abilities. Maybe he was an incubus in disguise. I giggled and sighed as my dream demon slowly rocked his hips against me, making sure to bury himself deeply with each thrust.

My hands flitted to my stomach, feeling the

distension every time he pushed my insides around.

I whispered that I loved him in my dreams, smiling as he whispered something in a tongue I couldn't recognize. But one thing was for sure, I felt every word with every thrust as I drifted back into the darkness of my mind.

EPILOGUE

KIMMY

"Get your disgusting little cretin hands off my counter!" he roared at a poor little boy who was picking his nose. "You, female! Get your blasted spawn away from me."

I slapped him with the back of my hand and he snarled in my face. "D, stop it. You're scaring the customers."

D was the same grumbly man I met the first day, in front of everyone. I enjoyed the fact that I was able to see the other side of him behind closed doors and that he reserved special treatment just for me.

After reassuring him that his true form didn't scare me but instead turn me on, he complained about the fact that he had to sneak away to the underworld more often to fix his 'flesh suit' without the master catching him. I still didn't know who this master was but I do hope he forgave D. He was such a good demon.

At least, good to me. I still didn't know where he went some nights, but he would come home full of adrenaline and desire. Who was I to question him if I reaped the benefits deliciously?

Today was a normal Thursday and soon after our shift began, two familiar faces showed up that I was not looking forward to seeing. My body tensed up as I watched my parents make their way toward The Good Char. I was nervous to say the least—scared too. D instantly noticed my change in composure and walked over, placing his warm hand on my shoulder to ask me if I was okay right as my parents made it to the counter.

I covered my face with both hands, almost wishing I could disappear. The grill was only a few feet away. Maybe D could...

There was an awkward short period of silence when my parents finally spoke.

"Well, Kimmy, we have good news for you. Cindy's mom called and she is home safe and sound."

I quickly dropped my hands from my face and began crying, leaking tears all over the counter. I was a nervous wreck. I couldn't tell them I already knew this. My heart was racing, worrying about where this conversation would lead. It was different arguing with my parents at home than in public. D grumbled and began spraying and cleaning the area in front of me when my father extended his hand.

"So, you are the famous Dick that my daughter has been raving on and on about."

I groaned. Did he really have to say that out loud? He was trying to embarrass me on purpose! I wasn't raving, just making sure they understood what an amazing person he was sans the fact that he was a demon.

D glared at him for a moment before confidently shaking his hand. I blushed like my whole body was being dipped into an oil vat. They both ignored me.

"I know you and my daughter are more than employee and owner," my dad gruffly said, trying to hide the words with a cough or two before quickly changing the subject. "This is a nice place you have here, *Dick.*"

"It's Dzik," D said nonchalantly but with a hint of firmness. I had to admit, it turned me on when he was mysterious like this.

"Well, let us get one of those dipped dogs everyone has been talking about," my father blustered as he puffed out his chest. What was going on right now?

D nodded silently as he personally dipped and fried two—one for both my parents. I wiped my face with the back of my hands and now I wanted to cry for another reason. How did I get so lucky with a man like him?

My father turned the food in his hand and

examined it while my mother, trying to bridge the weird tension in the air, dipped hers in ketchup and took the first brave bite.

"This is exquisite, Harold!" she exclaimed with the biggest smile on her face. "Hurry and take a bite. It's to die for."

"To die for, you say?" D smirked and chuckled.

I grimaced. I still didn't know what the secret batter was or why D would go missing once a week or so during our work week.

My dad finally took a bite and nodded his head in silence, not expressing one way or another if he liked it or not. My heart hammered inside of my chest. No matter what happens next, I wouldn't let him come between us. I laced my fingers in D's hand behind the counter and he gripped it firmly, calming me down.

Finally, my father cleared his throat and placed his corndog down on its paper tray. "Please, come talk a little business with me, Dick—If you have a moment."

D invited my father to the back leaving my mother and I standing at the front of The Good Char in silence.

DZIK

"Well, I'm going to cut right to the chase," Kimmy's sire continued. "This is a hell of an operation you have here. My little Kimmy means the world to me and I know she means a lot to you."

I braced myself for whatever threat was going to come out of his mouth. Kimmy would forgive me in time if I had to speed up her sire's demise. My phallus and I would make sure of it.

"So, how about a partnership?"

His expression, once hard, finally softened a few degrees. I didn't trust him. Why would I want to join forces with a human? Especially one that made my female sad when mentioned.

Kimmy was the only acceptable human in my existence. She was mine. This one I owed nothing to.

"Now just take a moment and think about it," he continued to coerce me. "We could open up several of your businesses all over, franchise it."

I mulled over his proposition. "Hmm."

I had never considered it. *I wonder how many demons I could get to come to the human realm to work for me? I would be the boss, their master... with multiple human servants beneath me. Yes. Yes, I liked this Idea.*

He extended his hand again in their human custom and I shook it. "So, there we have it. I'll get the papers for you and we can write up the contracts. You understand contracts right?"

He was testing me the same way I was testing him. The same way I tested Kimmy on her first day. The memory made my tail mentally swish.

"Of course," I said slowly as if he was the

simple one. "Buying and selling souls." I nodded with a chuckle. "If you've seen one contract, you've seen 'em all."

Two seconds of silence later, he slapped his knee and barked out a laugh while walking us back to the front. He was a strange one, but I wasn't surprised. He sired my little carrion, after all.

"This guy is a hoot, Margie. I like him. You have to bring him over for dinner."

Kimmy's sad eyes brightened when she saw me and my hidden tail wanted to thrash left and right at her attention. My cock wanted to feel her insides and without my control, my face broke into a smile for her.

"Okay, I promise," Kimmy immediately answered as her sire got on the other side of the counter. She waved at them without taking her eyes off me, blushing as she confidently walked into my arms.

It was a public claim she didn't do often enough. I would have to punish her later for that.

"One thing, Mr. Dzik," her mother piped in, watching our embrace closely then darting her eyes to Kimmy's stomach.

Yes, I was sure multiple spawns had already been planted in her womb. I made sure of it, nightly whether she was aware of it or not. I came home covered in blood one night to find her in peaceful slumber. I ravaged her in her sleep the way I always did, snickering when she mumbled the next day about starting her menstruation off schedule.

"You just have to give me your special recipe. I would love to bring some of this to my church for our special revival. Would you consider catering? Because I love your weiners!"

Kimmy choked as she buried her face against my chest while her mother smiled brightly and her father continued to scarf his down behind her.

Catering? More and more doors were opening up for me to continue wreaking havoc in the human realm.

Having a bunch of goody two-shoes eat human flesh at a place like that? I would make sure Zychor and Belchar heard about my evil deeds.

"I wouldn't miss it for the world," I told her with a wicked smile.

Thank you for reading *The Good Char*. If you want to check out some of my other books, then why not check out Obsideo's story in *The Hunger of Thieves*! https://books2read.com/u/mVeNxr

If you get your kicks in a magical manner, order toys from websites like bad dragon, and prefer your monsters *in* your bed instead of *under* them, then Y. D. is your girl.

Writing everything from spicy dark fantasy to fluffier-than-a-cool-marshmallow romance, Y.D. La Mar has her fingers in all sorts of man-meat pie, and the sky is the limit. Somehow, this magical mistress manages to balance her spicy author life with her responsibilities as a mom, a wife, and a resident of Sin City—*oh, irony, you've felled me.*

When the world is full of black-and-white, Y.D. plays in the grey zones, spending her time creating new ways to shock and awe her editor, as well as her readers.

Follow Me!

FLOWCODE
PRIVACY.FLOWCODE.COM

WANT UPDATES AND SNEAK PEEKS?

Sign up for my newsletter!

ALSO BY YD LA MAR

STREET ARRHYTHMIA TRILOGY

The Scent of Jasmine

For The Love of Import & Blood

To The Beat of The Streets

Spinoff

Arachnophilia

REVERSE HAREM

Warring Suns

The Truth Enslaved

SCI FI

The Essence of Esme

Deliverance (cowrite)

PARANORMAL

The Hunger of Thieves

Heart of The Reaper

Heart of the Reaper: Tales from the Underworld

Soul of The Reaper

Fate of The Reaper

Bury Me Alive

Lead Me Through The Fire

PSYCHOLOGICAL THRILLER

The Truth Enslaved

Actus Reus

CONTEMPORARY

The Formation of Us

The Conception of Us

The Revelation of Us

The House of Eden (cowrite)

When the Bloom Burns (cowrite)

OMEGAVERSE

Gero

Bernhard

Severin

DYSTOPIAN/POST APOCALYPTIC

We Are the Fallen

We Are the Guilty

MONSTER SHORT STORIES

Sinful Attraction

The Sky Below

Maeonia

Between Heaven and Earth

Fantasies Inflamed

Her 13th Hour

Ignus Fatuus

Suckers

Crimson Salt

ANTHOLOGIES

Used and Bound

Captured by Darkness

Until the End

After the Rain

Into The Woods

A Foster Fling

Bound by Monsters

Once Upon a Nightmare

Monsters in Love: Lost in the Dark

Monsters in Love: Lost in the Forest

Monsters in Love: Monstrous Ever After

Monsters in Love: Lost in the Deeps

Monsters in Love: Aloha Nui Loa

Monsters in Love: Lost in the Fire

Pollinators

The Red Key Club: Valentines Day Edition

The Red Key Club: Halloween Edition

Creepy Court

Crimson Vendetta

For the Love of Villains

SHARED WORLDS

Inferno World

Games of the Underworld

Rise of the Dreads

Monsters Ball

Rescue Me: A Hero Romance Collection